Time and Again

Henry Wood
Time and Again

by
Brian D. Meeks

Brian D. Meeks, Martelle, 52305
© 2013 by Brian D. Meeks
All rights reserved. Published 2013
Printed in the United States of America

5 4 3 2 1   19 18 17 16 15 14 13

ISBN: 978-0-9851046-2-7

This is a work of fiction. The characters, events, and story contained within, are created within the fertile imagination of the author. Any resemblance to persons, whether living or dead, or any events, are purely coincidental. Except for the cat, Buttons. The author had a cat very much like Buttons. Buttons was awesome.

No part of this publication may be reproduced in whole or in part, or stored in a retrieval system, or transmitted in any form, by any means electronic, mechanical, printing, photocopying, recording, chiseling in stone, or otherwise, without the written permission from the publisher, except for the inclusion of brief quotations in a review. For information regarding permission contact the publisher.

Time and Again

Chapter One

The radio was on. Music floated in the background while Henry relaxed with a bit of light hand planing on a piece of walnut. The last couple of months had been perfect. He had taken a few easy cases which kept him in the black: two wives wanting to know if their husbands were cheating on them, and a couple who needed him to find their daughter.

Henry had bad news for the one wife, and was pleased to inform the other that her man was simply taking dancing lessons – it was to be a surprise for their tenth anniversary. Both ladies cried at the news.

The daughter had run off with a guy who didn't have much money, but looked like James Dean. She came home after realizing that life with her rebel would not have a happy ending.

The song changed and Patty, Maxine, LaVerne, and their buddy, Bing Crosby, were asking the question, "Is you is or is you ain't my baby?" and it made Henry stop planing the piece of walnut. He set his old Stanley No. 5 on its side. The Philco 90 was on a table next to the closet door, and he reached over and turned up the volume.

It filled the woodworking shop with memories. Henry shuffled about in the sawdust, spinning around with a broom.

He wondered what Luna was doing. He had seen her only once

in the last couple of months. She had brought him cookies and they had eaten lunch and made promises to find the time to get together. He thought, *I should give her a call.*

The song faded, and Henry set the broom back up against the wall. His feet were still shuffling. The Philco played a catchy tune for Jell-O, and then a voice talked about the weather in Brooklyn.

Henry had gone back to working on the piece of walnut when the next song started - bom bom bom bom bom bom bom bom bom bom bom bom. Henry stopped. He didn't move. Those first notes crashed into his head, and as the Chordettes asked "Mr. Sandman" to bring them a dream, Henry felt a wave of time pull him back into the past.

The single had climbed up to #1 on the charts, and it seemed to be on the radio all the time. Henry didn't buy too many records, but he did have a record player. When the 45 showed up with a letter, he was caught off guard.

He didn't remember much about that day. Arriving at his office that morning, Henry had found the single and a letter, which someone had slid under the door. Opening the envelope and seeing the sender's name sent a chill down his spine. After reading it, he went home to his city apartment where he read it a hundred times more as the Chordettes sang.

As a rule, Henry stayed in the city only one night per week. Most days he preferred to head home to his house in Brooklyn. The house was quiet. Almost nobody knew that he had this second place, and this was where he did his woodworking and his best thinking.

The letter was from another time in his life. It hailed from the days before he was a detective, before he had closed himself off from all but a few of his closest friends. It was from a time when the world was at war, when there was a feeling of unity and purpose. It was from younger days. The handwriting was unmistakable, though he had only seen her scrawl once before.

That letter, too, had been read a hundred times.

Henry was not one for waxing nostalgic. In fact, he didn't talk about his past and rarely thought about anything but the present. For Henry, the best place to keep the past was out of sight and mind.

His best friend, "Big" Mike, loved to talk about the good old days. His newspaper buddy, Francis, when homesick for Paris, would drink, eat, tell tales of his youth, and continue on and on until he passed out. The last story would be entirely in French.

Henry didn't mind listening to others recount their glory days, but would change the subject when asked about his own. He had been this way since 1942.

The song faded. Henry turned off the radio and went upstairs. He took his jacket from the hall tree, removed the gloves from the pocket, and slid them on to his hands. As he headed out the door, he grabbed his fedora and ran a hand across the brim as he put it on. Music was a powerful trigger, and Henry felt that being alone at home wasn't as good as being alone anywhere else. The sound of the engine starting felt soothing, but it only nipped at the edges of the pain. Perhaps the drive would make him feel better.

Henry thought about suffering. This wasn't like having a cut or broken bone. It wasn't the sort of hurt which Mike had endured at the hands of Tommy "The Knife's" goons. It was, as a poet might say, bittersweet.

He turned left, then right, and finally got out of the neighborhood. Henry didn't think about where he was headed, but instinct took him into the city. The traffic wasn't too bad at that time of night. The lights of Manhattan were familiar; the sound of the wheels on the bridge seemed to sing the blues. It was as if somebody had plugged Henry's senses into a light socket. Bam! Sight and sound all mixed with the strange feeling deep down in his gut.

His car found its way to the apartment. He climbed up the

stairs, noticing that it was quieter than usual. The key in the lock seemed to echo in the silent hallway. Henry set the keys on the kitchen counter and went to the bookshelf. He removed the book she had given him, and let the two letters fall from its pages. He set the letters and book on the kitchen table and turned on his record player. The 45 of the Chordettes was still waiting, and he set the needle down carefully.

 Henry pulled out a bottle of vodka and placed two glasses across from one another. He poured a shot in each. Sitting down, he closed his eyes and picked up the first letter with his left hand, downed the shot, and opened his eyes to read again.

Chapter Two

Henry thought about the first time he saw her.
In 1942, Henry spent his days recovering from his less than heroic return from the war. At least, that's how he viewed it. The medals in his dresser drawer didn't change Henry's recollection of the events. Truth was sometimes a little murky. Each night he tried to erase the memory of his third night abroad. Each morning around 8:00 a.m., he would drag himself to the diner for breakfast before passing out for the day.
Her hair was long, straight, and dirty. She walked into the diner with a couple of other women who worked at the factory. He couldn't recall having seen a woman so filthy from head to toe who also glowed like a flawless diamond. They ordered breakfast, talked quietly, and seemed exhausted.
Was it the three extra cups of coffee that kept him from sleeping that day? He didn't think so.
That night, Henry had stayed home, skipped the bottle, and gone to sleep early. The next day, he shaved, put on his best suit, and picked up a *Wall Street Journal* before he went to the diner. Becky, the waitress who worried about Henry most mornings, was taken aback when she saw him. Henry played it cool and told her he was getting on with his life. He ate breakfast for two hours that

morning.

She didn't come in.

Three weeks later, Henry had gotten into a routine, found a job with a local P.I., and had mostly forgotten about the woman with the long hair. He was eating some toast when she sat down next to him at the counter.

Henry gave her a nod and she smiled. She was wearing a dress, had her hair all done up, and the grease had been replaced with makeup. She ordered a cup of coffee. When she had stirred in the cream for about five minutes, Henry asked if she was alright.

She had a voice that was deeper than he imagined...but not too deep. Her words had a bit of warmth to them. Her fiancé was going to ship out in a week, and she was taking the train to D.C. to see him one last time before he left. She said that the train didn't leave for four hours, but she was so excited that she just had to get ready and wait.

He remembered how she talked about her beloved. He had envied the young man waiting for her in D.C. because, if for no other reason, her dark brown eyes were so in love.

Now, Henry took another shot of vodka. He could imagine her with the chiseled cheek bones, button nose, and those piercing eyes, sitting across the table. It hurt to think about her.

Henry stood up from the table and walked around the room. Her face was firmly fixed in his mind. She wasn't the love of his life...that painful wound belonged to another memory. She was something, though. Henry took a hit from the bottle and stood looking out of the window. The cars rolled past. A woman chased her bonnet making an attempted getaway. A police officer was giving directions to an elderly couple. Henry noticed a man lighting up a cigarette with a cabbie on the corner, but as he turned away from the window, there she was again, in his mind, walking around his soul and bumping into all of the bottled up emotions he had hidden away. If she wasn't careful, she might knock one over and let those feelings spill out. That wouldn't do at all.

He was more tired than drunk. Back in the day, Henry really knew how to crawl into a bottle, but it seemed that those days might have passed, too. He didn't go to bed, though; he lay down on the couch and put his arm across his eyes. He tried to shut out the dim light from the street and the burning light of her face in his mind's eye. He wondered if she realized the pain she had inflicted when sending him the record.

She was the kindest person he knew. It seemed unlikely that she envisioned him spending months being torn to shreds emotionally when he failed to find her. It just wasn't her way.

His mind retrieved a happier moment. It was the day they spent looking at early works of art by Henri Matisse. Henry didn't care much for art, until he saw it through her eyes. She talked with ease about Matisse's first paintings. Henry didn't understand much of what she was saying, but he never dismissed art again. In fact, there were many times, over the years, when he found himself drawn into a museum for comfort. The quiet appealed to him. Eventually he started to enjoy the paintings, too.

Art wasn't the only mark she had left on his life. She had taught him to dream. When they would meet, usually at the diner, the conversation would often be about what was to come. She talked about the family she would raise with her fiancé when he returned from saving the world. What Henry found most endearing is that the dream constantly changed. The names of the children were never the same. The houses moved from the city to the country and all around the world. Even her plans for the big wedding were a work in progress.

She did have one constant, and that was the dress. Henry loved hearing her describe it. She knew every detail and would blush when realizing that she was going on about it, again. Henry always told her to continue, which she gladly did.

She was simple and complex, light and dark, day and night, and more than anything, she was unlike anyone he had ever met, before or since.

Her memory brought Henry such pain mixed with joy...he couldn't bring himself to utter her name. He thought about saying it, just once, but held his tongue.

Just as he was fading off to sleep, he cursed his radio, for it, really, was the one that poured the salt into his wound.

If Henry had not had the radio on, he would have remained at home. He might have still been in his shop when the flash of light and loud pop came from his closet. He would have noticed the new "present" left for him in the strange closet.

He may have been able to stop what was about to happen.

Chapter Three

While Henry slept, his old mentor was celebrating just ten blocks away.

Michael Thomas Moore, named for the poet, gave Henry his start in the private detective business. Now he was nearing the end of his days of stakeouts, crappy food, and sleeping in his car with the Leica camera on the seat next to him.

Everyone called him "Mickey." He taught Henry to pick a lock, trail a suspect, and always have friends on the force. Mickey would say things like, "The clients always lie," or "If the retainer is too generous, the job is too dangerous," and "Never forget your notebook... and write down everything."

Mickey had shown Henry the art of observation. They had spent hour upon hour just watching people. If they weren't on a case, Mickey was teaching him to see his surroundings. At any moment, Mickey would ask, "What color hat was the woman we just passed wearing?" If Henry didn't know, it would cost him lunch. Henry didn't make a lot of money back then, so he had to learn fast, or Mickey would eat up his entire paycheck.

The Dublin Rogue had darts, a pool table, peanuts and pretzels on the bar, half a dozen booths, and a perpetually sticky floor. A hangout for the local beat cops, this had become a favorite of

Mickey's twenty years before. There were few people who could remember a day when he wasn't perched in his favorite spot. The bar had opened shortly after Prohibition ended, and not long after Mickey had become a fixture.

"The next round is on me!" Mickey said, as he raised his drink.

Everyone in the bar cheered. The waitress and bartender, though surprised, started handing out the beers. Three of New York's men in blue from the ninth precinct were giving Mickey a hard time about his largess. "I must really be plastered, did I hear that correctly? Mickey is finally buying a round!"

"I'm celebrating,

Mr. Thompson...er, sorry, Officer Thompson. I can see the light at the end of the tunnel, and it isn't a train," Mickey shot back triumphantly. He had known Bobby Thompson since he was a young boy trying to sneak into the bar. Mickey never got used to the idea of him being a full-fledged peace officer.

The short, round officer called Carl added, "You come in ta some dough, Mickey?"

The tall, thin sergeant, who everyone called Slim, said, "What's the story, Mic? You finally going to sail off into the sunset?"

Mickey had been telling everyone about his dream of buying a boat for years. He planned on sailing to Florida, opening a bar, spending his days on the beach, and his nights serving and drinking Mai Tais. Those who frequented the bar knew his dream by heart. They could describe the pool table in the corner, name the specials on Tuesday, and picture his vision as if it were a photo hanging on the wall.

He had developed a reputation for being a bit of a tightwad, which was true. Mickey had been living like a bum, which suited him, for thirty years. He saved every penny and knew exactly how much he needed.

Mickey took a long pull of his beer. "As you know, I have been looking forward to the day when I can sail off into the sunset and leave you rascals behind. This morning, I took my last job. Two weeks, three tops, and I will be done with this racket! By June first, I should be ready to head south."

"Cheers to Mickey!"

The waitress gave Mickey a kiss on the cheek, handed him another beer, and said, "Congrats, old man."

Mickey asked her to sail away with him and then smacked her on the bottom.

"Can you even get your mainsail up?" she said with a wink. Those within earshot howled with laughter.

Everyone stopped over to pat Mickey on the back, ask him to describe his boat - just one more time - or just to thank him for the beer. After an hour or so, Mickey grabbed his hat and stepped out into the night to start his last job. The sky had opened up and a cold rain was pounding the pavement. Mickey yelled good-bye, held the day's newspaper over his head, and jogged to his car. The bar crowd gave him a cheer as he left.

Chapter Four

Bam! Bam! Bam!

The pounding on the door shook Henry from his dream. Nearly falling off the couch, he yelled, "What?"

"My name is Officer Brently. May I come in? There has been an accident."

Henry opened the door and held it for Officer Brently, "What sort of accident?"

"It looks like a hit and run, but that is not why I'm here. I was sent by Thompson; he said you should get down here right away. The vic is..." his voice trailed off. Officer Bentley had a habit of speaking very quickly realized the gravity of the situation. "The man who was killed is your friend Mickey."

Henry was stunned. He hadn't talked to Mickey in a couple of years and, suddenly, he was gone. "What happened?"

"I was told to bring you down to the scene. I'll tell you along the way."

Henry grabbed his overcoat and hat and didn't bother to lock the door behind him. The officer explained that Mickey had been hit after leaving The Dublin Rogue. It had just happened, and he had rushed over to get Henry. Officer Bentley gave his condolences and said that everyone who knew Mickey loved him. That was all there was to say, so they walked through the chilly night in silence. Henry's mind raced. He checked to see if he had his notebook. He did. The memories of Mickey's teachings seemed to flood back to him. Henry remembered the saying Mickey used daily: "There are no coincidences and accidents are seldom accidental." Henry picked up the pace of his stride.

After six blocks they rounded the corner. The lights of the squad cars cut through the dark and damp. The street was wet and lined with cars; a few lights on in the buildings. A crowd of people stood outside of the bar. Henry passed from the sidewalk to the street through a gap in the parked cars. He was greeted by Officer Carl whom Henry had known since he was a boy. The look on Carl's face was of profound sadness. He had loved Mickey like a father much like Henry did. "It was raining pretty hard, and it looks like the driver didn't see him. We were inside, and a couple who left a few minutes after Mickey found him."

"The driver didn't stop?"

"Nope, looks like a hit and run. We are going to canvas the neighborhood and find out if anyone saw anything, but, with the rain, I doubt anyone could have seen much. Maybe if they happened to be looking, a make and model, but I don't know."

Henry didn't have anything to say. He walked over to the body, lifted the corner of the sheet, and looked at his friend. The peaceful look on Mickey's face seemed out of place. Henry expected anguish or terror but didn't find it. He badly wanted Mickey to offer him one more rule to live by. Something inane that would bring comfort at this exact moment. The noise from the city and the crowd seemed to fade away. Those who were standing about gave Henry and Mickey a moment to be alone.

This made it easier for Henry to slip Mickey's notebook out of his breast pocket. He took the pen as well not because it was important but because Henry knew that the pen without the notebook might draw attention.

"Always think about how things go together," popped into Henry's head. Promises were taken seriously by Mickey, and he had instilled this in Henry. He could hear Mickey clear as a bell. He was still speaking to him. Henry covered Mickey back up and stood slowly. "I hear you. I will find out who did this."

The rain was still falling though it had slowed. Henry walked up the street to the spot where he had crossed from the sidewalk. He stood there. The emptiness was out of place. He looked up and down the street. The rest of the street was lined with cars bumper to bumper. This spot was just five cars behind where Mickey had parked. Henry looked down at the pavement. A tiny stream of rainwater passed across the middle of the spot. Against the rear tire of the car in front, water was pooling. Henry looked closer.

A small wet pile of cigarette butts gathered between the edge of the tire and the curb. Henry walked up the street a ways. The rest of the gutter was wiped clean from the hard rain. Somebody had been sitting in their car smoking, and, by the number of cigarettes, they had been there a long time. This wasn't a hit and run. It was murder.

Henry's hand went to his coat pocket just to check that Mickey's notebook was still there. He pulled out his own notebook, counted the wet butts, and noted it. He counted the number of cars parked on the street and wrote down the license plates of the ones surrounding Mickey's car.

Henry walked home slowly. Mickey's words followed him: "Life is short; do what you love; and never have regrets." Mickey said this while placing a bet on a horse. He lost the bet but loved the action. "All women are trouble except for one. The hard part is finding the one." This was the wisdom Mickey passed along after Henry had gotten the first letter. It hadn't made him feel any better. In fact, it made him feel worse. "Pain is sweetest when it is from a crazy and beautiful girl." This was sort of said, sort of slurred while Mickey was drowning his sorrows after his longtime, part-time love interest had finally given up on him.

Now he was gone. Henry was filled with regret at not having stayed in touch. He knew Mickey wouldn't approve of his feelings and would likely say, "Don't cry for me; drink a toast and be done with it. Plus, crying is for girls or guys who are drunk. And you aren't drunk yet."

Henry wasn't drunk though he wanted to be. He wished he had drank more vodka earlier in the evening. The ten-block walk home wasn't long enough. He went right past the stairs to his apartment and continued on into the city night. The last few hours had been devastating.

"Damn you, Kat!" he said out loud and regretted it soon after. He hadn't said her name in years and had fought off the temptation earlier when he was wallowing in self-pity. She snuck past his lips, and the sound of her name ripped through him.

Katarina, who had been named for Katherine the Great, by her mother who loved history. She was well liked by Mickey. He often told Henry to stop being her friend and start being a man. Henry never listened and had let her slip away without ever telling her how he felt. He had assumed she knew, but how would she have known? Now Mickey was gone, and her memory was back.

He wandered into the diner. It was 4 am, and Becky was there as she always seemed to be. She had aged some since he last saw her, but her smile was still a comfort. "Henry Wood, good to see you. I just put a pot of coffee on. I will have a plate of eggs and toast up for you in a jiffy." Nothing much had changed here, and it felt like an old, warm blanket around Henry's shoulders.

Henry hung his coat on the hook by the door and shook the rain off his hat and set it on the counter. The sound of the coffee cup being set in front of him was like the bell at a boxing match. It was time to get to work. Round one was beginning. Henry flipped open Mickey's notebook.

* * *

Across town, in a dimly lit room, a figure sat alone in a high backed chair. The fireplace sent warmth throughout the room as the solitary figure stared into the flames, wondering where the years had gone. The hair, no longer blond, but more of a stately gray, still looked good. The eyes, piercing blue, saw more than most. They saw the possibilities, the future... a different world.

On the coffee table, next to the Tiffany lamp, a copy of Plutarch's Moralia was opened to a favorite passage. The cup of tea was cold, barely touched. In the hallway, the muffled sound of a door knocker bounced off the walls. The figure didn't move to answer the door, as it was beneath him to do so. There were other people for such tasks.

The delicate footsteps of Mrs. Hock could be heard coming from the kitchen.

There were whispers at the door, then two sets of footsteps approached and stopped. A pause, and then the door slowly opened and a shaft of light crept across the floor, not wanting to be a bother.

"Herr Doctor, Mr. Mauer has arrived. He apologizes for the lateness of the hour, but he would like to give you an update."

Hans Mauer, a six-foot-three-inch block of granite, was light on his feet and surprisingly stealthy, when it was a necessity. He had been with Dr. Schafer for eight years. Hans was often given tasks which most people would find menial, but he never appeared to mind. He would go to the grocery for Mrs. Hock, mostly because she was the scariest five-foot-four-inch German woman he had ever met. He was sure she could stare down a Panzer division with nothing but a rolling pin and her angry face.

Hans also served as a foil for Dr. Schaeffer when he needed to play some chess. Mostly, though, he would stand behind his boss on those rare occasions when he was out in public or conducting business. Dr. Schaeffer was quite sure people were far less likely to try to cheat him when Hans was in tow. He was right. Hans was a jack of all trades.

The doctor stood and greeted Hans warmly. "How are you tonight, my friend?"

"I am fine, Doctor. I apologize for the late hour, but I had a number of things to take care of and it took much longer than I anticipated." Hans shook the doctor's hand and took the other seat in front of the fire. They spent many hours here talking, planning, or sometimes just enjoying silence.

"I hope my request wasn't too much of an inconvenience. It was a necessity, however, and I do appreciate your efforts."

Hans took out a piece of folded paper. He read it once, checking for errors in spelling, though he knew there wouldn't be any opportunity to fix them, should he find any problems. Dr. Schaeffer, an incredibly precise man, demanded perfection of himself, but wasn't as critical of those around him. He couldn't imagine anyone being as precise as him, and, as such, always expected flaws. Hans was exceptional, however, and frequently surprised Dr. Schaeffer. On these occasions, he would stop, look at Hans, and then genuinely express his gratitude.

Hans handed the neatly folded piece of paper to his boss. He read it slowly, then stood and placed it in the fire. They both watched it burn, and said nothing until Mrs. Hock returned with a bottle of Pierre Ferrand cognac.

"Will you join us Mrs. Hock?" asked the doctor, as he always did. Mrs. Hock declined, as it wouldn't be proper.

The two men sat with the brandy snifters in their hands, slowly warming the liquor, and staring into the fire.

Life was good for both of these men. But it is man's nature to want more. They each had dreams, which neither shared entirely, but could sense in the other.

The flames began to die down. Hans stood and gave the doctor a nod, then saw himself out. The doctor, as was his custom on many nights, drifted off in his favorite chair.

Hans turned up the collar on his overcoat and walked through the cold early morning streets, thinking about what was beginning. He would not be able to sleep for several more hours, he knew it, so he did what came naturally. He walked.

Chapter Five

At 4:00 a.m. a massive man in a silk robe began his routine. Andre Garneau, a man of inherited means, was, by most accounts, a bastard. Those who called him such, were usually people who didn't know him well, or were naturally predisposed to being charitable. It was likely that if Monsieur Garneau were asked, he, too, would have considered himself a bastard, and would likely have answered with a hint of pride in his voice.

A French maid in an embarrassingly short skirt and silk stockings ran a warm bath in the claw-foot bathtub. She made her exit when the tub was full lest she witness him disrobing. She made his bed, laid out his attire for the morning, and then went to help or, more accurately, hide in the kitchen with the cook. Upon hearing the thundering sounds of Andre's massive feet descending the stairs, she would sneak up the back stairs to start her day's cleaning. Most of the rest of the day, the outfit which left little to the imagination was only seen by the chauffeur, and then it was often lying on the floor.

His name was Claude. He had been the driver for five years and found the perks of his job were worth the grief given by his employer. Claude was tall, painfully handsome, not so bright, and completely devoid of ambition. He was exactly the type of person which Monsieur Garneau liked to surround himself with. Andre was not a trusting person. He believed that those who possessed ambition and drive were, by their nature, crooks and thieves. Just to be sure, he paid them slightly more than they could find anywhere else. He considered it a cheap insurance policy against loss and change, two things he abhorred.

At precisely 5:30 a.m., Andre was joined by his personal assistant, just as he was finishing his breakfast. Arthur, a Brit who grew up in Paris, was the only staff member who didn't live in the king's castle, but maintained his own tiny apartment a few blocks away. He was also the only royal subject who was able to say "no" to the rotund tyrant. Arthur was an artist who found that starving didn't coexist well with his love of gourmet food.

He had met Andre on a day which was unusual for two reasons. One, Andre was visiting a Parisian gallery showing a minor artist, something he rarely did. In general, Andre would only leave his abode for the topmost luminaries of the art world. The second reason the day was unusual was because Andre's mood could have been described as "joyful."

The two men struck up a conversation about art, which soon led to dinner, two bottles of wine…and an invitation to become Andre's personal assistant.

Arthur put down his brushes and picked up a silver fork.

The name Andre Garneau was known throughout the art world. In less than a decade, he had built both one of the most impressive collections on display in a Manhattan home, and a second collection which was tucked away in a private room and never shown to anyone. This second collection contained works which were often purchased from people who had acquired them by unsavory means. Andre's paranoia about being cheated made him cautious, but since he was also born sans conscious, he never inquired as to how a work was obtained. If a painting or sculpture's providence could be proven, then Andre could be counted upon to pay well, by black market standards, in order to secure the treasure.

As Andre soaked in the tub this day, he thought about his latest quest. It would be the prize of his secret collection, and each time he thought about placing it among his other treasures, his heart started to race. The community of serious art collectors was a small one, and the subset who also maintained "private" collections was even more exclusive. Monsieur Garneau's collection was among the finest of the shadow collectors, but it was not the undisputed premier collection.

That distinction went to a ghost, known by the moniker "Falcon." The Falcon would swoop in and pluck the finest morsels from the best underground private auctions, via phone. He worked through brokers who never met him, either. The Falcon was known for having platinum credit. He paid promptly, usually in precious metals or diamonds, and it was rumored that his pockets were so deep that, were one to drop a coin into them, it would fall for days.

Andre relaxed in the warm water and imagined the envy the Falcon would feel when he learned of he'd been bested.

The ringing of a tiny silver bell indicated that breakfast was nearly ready. Andre pulled himself out of the bath, dried himself, and got dressed. For such a large man, he did have an impeccable sense of fashion. The last part of his pre-breakfast routine was to brush his hair and check the mirror for any follicle which might dare be out of place. His hair feared him almost as much as the staff and rarely misbehaved.

The kitchen smelled of bacon, eggs, toast, and various pastry goodies. A bakery two blocks north would deliver a dozen delectable items each morning, exactly five minutes before the tiny bell was rung. The quality of the pastry had been so pleasing to Andre's palate that he had commissioned twelve items per day, anything the bakery wished to create.

The pastry chef was the only person who Andre truly respected. He called him the "Caravaggio of the croissant." Over the previous five years, Andre had politely given feedback, mostly positive, about each of their daily creations. He was fair, kind, and incredibly detailed in his pastry editorials. Each night, Andre would write a one page note to the chef. It would be given to the delivery boy, who treated it as if it were a Dead Sea Scroll. The boy, careful not to wrinkle or crease the note in any way, then delivered it to his boss. Andre's insights into the sugary treats were so profound that the pastry chef took each comment as if it had come from a holy pastry monk.

Arthur arrived on time. He took a seat across from Andre, as was his daily custom, and waited until he was asked for the progress report. The cook set a plate of sausage, eggs, and toast in front of Arthur. He would wait to eat until after he had given his report.

Two minutes of relative silence later, Andre looked up, dabbed his face with his napkin, and gave Arthur a nod.

"I have an update. You aren't going to like it."

Chapter Six

Henry sat and nibbled at his breakfast. He was hungry, but distracted. He was heartsick at Mickey's untimely death. The internal motor that lay dormant most of the time started up, and his instincts began to crowd out the pain. He would focus on finding Mickey's killer. He could grieve later.

The notebook he lifted from Mickey would take time. He looked at the chicken scratches, which sometimes resembled words, and gave a smile as he remembered an afternoon not long after he had been taken under Mickey's wing. Traffic was horrible in midtown that day. Mickey was trying to get to a building adjacent to Central Park. He had a client who lived there and would let him park in the building when he had business in the neighborhood. As it turned out, there was a long-legged, twenty-something blonde who had been promoted from secretary to the wife of an elderly oil tycoon, who might be showing up at the same building.

The oil tycoon suspected, or more aptly, assumed it was likely, she was having an affair. They had been married for two years, and though she still looked good on his arm, her youth and general stupidity had taken their toll on his affection for her. Two years older, wiser, and closer to his final carriage ride, the gentleman had started to think about his legacy. He hired Mickey to get proof that she was stepping out on him.

"Everything alright, honey?" Becky asked as she filled up Henry's cup of coffee.

Henry smiled. "Just thinking about a friend."

"I noticed the smile on your face. First one of the morning I've seen." She gave him a wink and went to take the order of a young couple who were holding hands in the corner booth.

Henry looked at the notebook and fell back into his interrupted memory.

"Hey kid, you payin' attention?! The devil's in the details!" Mickey had hollered at him as they parked the car. Henry remembered him always asking if he was listening.

Henry hung on every word.

They walked across the street to the park. Mickey handed Henry the notebook and said, "Read me what I've written there."

Henry couldn't make out a single coherent sentence. It seemed to be all gibberish.

"The reason you can't read it is I have my own sort of shorthand. It's like a code. Do you know why I do that?"

Henry chuckled to himself as he remembered his answer.

"Because you are nuts?" He had said it sort of sheepishly, with a hint of confusion, and a smidgen of annoyance.

Mickey had laughed hard and long. But then he said that it was because he had a reputation for keeping secrets. Clients liked to know that their business stayed their business. He went on to explain how he had developed his shorthand over the years, sometimes using code words, other times a substitution cipher, and on occasion drawing a tiny picture which would remind him of something.

Henry looked back at the notebook and flipped through the last three pages. He could tell the previous case had ended four pages before, as the writing stopped halfway, had two bold lines drawn across it, and a lengthy number below them. Those numbers, actually just the middle five, could be found on a file folder in a locked cabinet in Mickey's office. Mickey always wrote a detailed report, mostly for himself, and filed it after the case was done. Those reports were in plain English. Mickey was not eloquent in his writing, but he was thorough. The problem, as Henry saw it, was that Mickey never updated the files until after the case was closed. Henry hadn't seen him in a while, so it was possible he had changed his ways, but Henry suspected that the adage about "old dogs and new tricks" made it unlikely. Still, he would check the office later today, just to be sure.

The persistent memory returned as Henry was fishing out some bills to pay the receipt Becky had set by his plate.

Mickey and Henry had bought a newspaper. They were sitting on a bench. It gave them a view of the building where the suspected wayward blonde might be stopping off to meet a roguishly good-looking janitor from Cuba. Mickey had sketched a hand palm, a rectangle 217, and a football in his notebook, followed by "10 J 14 15 4 20 over/under 84 and chain." After Mickey had asked Henry what it meant and then made him go buy two hot dogs from the vendor, he explained each part.

"The palm reminds me of a cop directing traffic. So it means "stop". The rectangle is a building and 217 the number. I usually remember the street, so I don't include it. The point is to take enough notes so I am able to recreate a mental picture. The football is not really a football, but it looks like one, so it might fool people. To me, it looks like an eyeball, so it means 'watch'. Next is the client's name. 'Jones' is coded using the alphabet 1 - 26 as a substitution cipher. But I get clever. The first letter is J, and is a 10. That is how I know where I started. Then the next number is a 14, which is actually one number above the letter I really want. If someone tries to just do the substitution, they get the letter 'N,' not the letter 'O'. The next number will be one below the letter I really want. It goes back and forth until I finish the name.

"The 'over/under' serves two purposes. It tells me which substitution cipher I used on the word before and it reminds me of a basketball, or more accurately a ball. The words 'and chain' is just 'and chain'. So…what did I write?"

Henry answered his quirky teacher with, "Stopped at Building 217 to watch Jones's ball and chain."

"That's right!" Mickey answered. "But you didn't get me any relish." And he handed the hot dog back to Henry.

Henry closed the notebook and the memory. He said goodbye to Becky and started his long walk to Mickey's old office.

Chapter Seven

Henry walked past the front entrance of the familiar building. He went around to the alley and entered through the nondescript door. This led to a long thin hallway, with a couple of small offices and a large closet for the custodial staff.

At the end of this hallway, behind another door, was a stairway. The "back stairs" went up to the fifth floor without any stops in between. It was a strange design element, to be sure. Mickey had loved it.

When the building was constructed, the owner, a paranoid investment banker, had insisted upon the secret stairs being included in the design. His offices occupied the top floor, which was unfortunate in October of '29 when he jumped out the window and hit an awning on the first floor, which broke his fall enough to prevent his death. He was in excruciating pain for the month-long hospital stay. Happily, he did recover, got out of the investment business, and lived out his remaining days living off his rental, in the very building which refused to do him in. When he died, his office, with the secret stairway, was rented to Mickey.

Mickey accepted all sorts of clients. Some of his female clients asked Mickey to find out if their husbands were cheating on them. Usually they were, and Mickey always found out.

Mickey explained the back stairs to Henry like this: "We do our job. Sometimes our job makes people unhappy. I usually hear them coming, so the back stairs allow me to make a tactical retreat. They usually only have enough steam for one encounter. After that, they get a divorce or patch things up with their ladies. Either way, nobody gets hurt."

Henry smiled as he climbed the stairs. It was narrow, and each floor had a window which looked out on the alley. The windows were covered in grime, as the custodial staff never bothered with the secret stairs. When Henry got to the top, there was a slight landing and a door. It was locked. Henry took out his picks and let himself into Mickey's office.

The sound of the door closing behind him and the hollow echo it made struck a painful chord. The familiar was usually a comfort, except after the loss of a friend and mentor. Now it just stung.

Henry sat down behind the desk. It was cluttered with papers, racing forms, three coffee cups, and the March issue of Sport magazine. It featured Rocky Marciano on the cover, with the heading "Man of the Year." There was an article about Leo Durocher, too, and a listing of the "U.S. College Coaches Select Basketball's All-Time All-Americans." The look on Marciano's face seemed fake to Henry, like he was trying to act tough for the camera. Henry thought about how he was putting on a face now, while he looked for the man who ran down his friend.

Mickey loved boxing, almost as much as he loved baseball and betting the ponies. Though it was the current issue, the magazine had a worn look. No doubt it had been curled up and carried on a stakeout or two, joined him for lunch, and been read front to back several times. That is how Mickey did things. If he liked an article after he read it, he would mull it over for a while, then read it again. Mickey could almost see through the pages, right into the mind of the journalist, sitting ringside, taking notes. He could imagine the sights, sounds and smells of the match, as if he were in the squared circle himself. The writers who tried to bring all the senses into play, those were his favorites. It wasn't enough to know that the arena was smoke-filled - Mickey wanted his eyes to burn and to taste the cigars as he read.

Henry flipped through the pages and then tossed it back on the desk. He leaned back in Mickey's chair and tried to get into his old teacher's mind. Henry opened the notebook and looked at the last page, hoping to find a starting place, but he didn't do any better than he had at the diner. He looked in the right desk drawer and saw one of Mickey's lock pick sets. The leather case, worn from years of riding around in Mickey's pocket, sat there waiting for action.

Henry was taken back to his second week on the job. Mickey had called him into the office. Henry stood before the desk, cluttered in much the same way as it was now, and Mickey opened the very same right drawer and took out two sets of lock picks, the worn one and a brand new set, which he gave Henry.

"Sit down, let me explain how these work. You're going to need to get into places where people would rather you didn't. These are your skeleton keys, as it were. Always keep them with you." He chuckled. Sometimes Mickey would laugh at things he said, just because. Some old inside joke, which he rarely shared.

After a short while of explaining how they worked, he had Henry practice on the secret door. It took Henry a while to get it right, but he finally got the hang of that lock. For the next week, Henry took the back stairs, up to the office, and opened the locked door with his picks. Mickey then had him try the three locks on the front door. Mickey had three different styles of locks, so it was a greater challenge. Another week and Henry had those down pat, too.

One morning, a few weeks later, Mickey made the coffee before Henry arrived. This was unusual, as he generally asked Henry do it first thing. They sat and talked. It was relaxed; Mickey didn't quiz him on anything, just two guys shooting the breeze. They finished one pot and Mickey made another. Henry was enjoying his bonding moment with his boss. Mickey had gotten up, said he was going to "meet a man about a horse," and told Henry to wait there, as he was expecting a call. Henry sat there and drank his coffee while the boss visited the restroom.

When Mickey got back, he poured himself a tall glass of water, which was also unusual. The sound of the water made Henry realize he needed to excuse himself. "Sure thing, sport," Mickey said with a strange smile. Henry walked down the hall and slammed his face into the men's room door. Mickey had locked it. Henry called Mickey a bastard, ran back to get his picks, and then fumbled with the lock on the bathroom door for what seemed like a thousand years. When he got back to the office, that door was locked, too.

Henry learned Mickey's lesson about always having his picks handy, and the value of being able to work quickly. The next day Henry had to make the coffee again. Henry substituted salt for sugar in Mickey's cup.

Now the office was quiet, though still buzzing with the memories of lessons past. Henry hoped he could find some evidence for the current case, something which would start him out on the right track.

The ringing of the phone was unexpected. He let it ring once, then Henry answered, as he always had, "Michael Thomas Moore Detective Agency".

There was a long pause. Henry could hear faint breathing, and she spoke. Henry knew the voice. And she knew his.

Chapter Eight

"Henry, is that you?" came the familiar and surprised voice.

"It is. How are you, Katarina?" Henry said, with a sudden calm born out of surprise, confusion, and a sick feeling in his stomach.

"I didn't expect...er, I mean...I called for Mickey. You went out on your own, didn't you? I left the record at Henry Wood Detective Agency a while back...I assumed that was you." Her voice returned to normal, as did her composure.

"I did, and I got the record, thank you. I have enjoyed it. That office had a little mishap a couple of months back. I am in the Flatiron building now. Your note and the gift was quite a surprise. Why didn't you come back and say " 'hello'"?" Henry asked. He had a thousand other questions, but none of them came to him at that moment.

"I didn't want to be a bother," she said. "I was only in town for the day. Have you been well?" She asked it with all the grace and confidence Henry remembered.

"No. Last night, Mickey was killed...I don't think it was an accident."

There was a long pause, then, "I am so sorry, Henry."

"Thanks. So what is it you needed Mickey to do? Are you in trouble?"

"Oh, it was nothing...."

It struck Henry as strange, but he didn't have time to dig deeper: there was a light knocking at the office door.

"Just a minute, Katarina, there's someone at the door." Henry set the phone down and opened the left desk drawer. He pulled out Mickey's back up revolver and gave it a check. The gun was loaded. He tucked it into his waistband behind his back, and went to answer the door.

The door was locked, naturally, so Henry started undoing each one – and heard some shuffling outside. Had the person been trying to look through the key hole? When he opened the door, there stood a small older gentleman, with his hat in hand.

He nodded politely at Henry, but said nothing.

"Please come in," Henry said, holding the door.

Henry believed in being cautious. He had no idea what the little man wanted, but he wasn't going to take any chances. It could be something quite innocent, just a man looking for a detective, who knew nothing of Mickey's demise. On the other hand, the man taking off his hat might be mixed up in it somehow. Either way, Henry wanted to size him up.

He was holding a briefcase and dressed in a brown suit. He looked as if he was the sort of person who always wore a brown suit.

Henry stuck out his hand. "My name is Henry, I'll be happy to help you in a minute. I was in the middle of a call when you knocked."

"Of course, I shall take a seat and wait. Don't feel you need to hurry on my account."

Henry walked into the office, making sure to avoid turning his back on the man in brown. Henry didn't want to frighten him, as some might find the sight of the gun...upsetting. Henry closed the door to Mickey's office. He picked up the phone hoping to find out a bit more about why Katarina had wanted to talk to Mickey.

"Sorry about that; it's a small man in a brown suit, who is looking for Mickey, too. Why did you say you wanted to talk to him?"

"I didn't say, but perhaps you could help me out. Shall we meet for dinner?"

Henry knew she was avoiding his question. He could worry about Katarina later, so he agreed. He suggested a place they both knew, hung up the receiver, and took a deep breath.

Henry didn't feel comfortable taking a meeting, while sitting at his departed friend's desk, so he grabbed a yellow pad of paper and returned to the waiting room.

The man stood up and handed Henry a business card with some writing on it. Henry read it.

"Please call me, or stop by. It is urgent." It was written in Mickey's scrawl.

Henry flipped the card over and recognized the familiar card of his mentor.

The man spoke clearly and with purpose. "As this is Mickey's Detective Agency, and you introduced yourself as Henry, and the fact that you were in his office, speaking on his phone, I will infer that he is not in."

"That is correct..." Henry started to say, but was interrupted by the man in brown.

"I do not know why I was summoned, but my time is valuable, and if you know what the meaning of this is, do, please, get on with it."

It was obvious by his tone that the man was not aware of what had happened, so Henry decided to see if he could get anything useful out of him.

"Mickey is not available at the moment. I don't work for him, but I used to. I am filling in for him and just started to try to get a handle on his cases. I apologize for this horrible inconvenience, but his inability to be here was unavoidable. May I ask what business you are in?"

"I am a man of considerable means. I have many real estate holdings here in the city, and I'm a collector of art." He paused, sensing that his tone had been rather abrupt before, and he appreciated how polite Henry had been. "I am sorry, if I was short with you. I've had several meetings today and was hoping to quickly take care of this 'supposedly' urgent business."

Henry didn't have much to go on, so he just went with his gut.

"Again, I must apologize. Mickey has several cases at the moment. If I may have your card, I'll call you later, but only if it's necessary. I can assure you, Mickey is not the sort of person to waste the time of an important man, such as yourself."

This courtesy seemed to please the man in the brown suit. He handed Henry his card, placed his hat on his head, and smiled before he walked out the door. Henry tucked the card into Mickey's notebook and, after looking around a bit more, left too.

Chapter Nine

Henry locked up the office he once loved. Now, it seemed lonely. If he hung out there much longer, the memories of Mickey would likely wring out the last ounce of energy he could marshal.

This wouldn't do at all. He needed to get home, take a shower, and make it to his office. Henry was sure he would be able to clear his head sitting at his own desk.

The walk home was chilly and wet. He climbed the stairs and remembered he hadn't locked the door this morning . This worried him a little…but not a lot. Henry's mind wasn't firing on all cylinders. The thought that his door was unlocked was so unimportant as to be laughable, yet, as he trudged up the stairs, he worried.

Pausing before the door, he took a breath and opened it.

The door swung closed behind him.

Everything was fine.

Henry took a shower. He put on one of his nicer suits – not his nicest, as he would need that for the funeral.

Mickey didn't have any family. Henry once asked him if he ever thought about marriage. Mickey had answered, "Yes, but I can usually get over it with a good stiff drink."

Mickey's parents had lived their entire lives in Kenmare County,

Kerry, Ireland. They had met when his mother's parents moved to town. She was six and he was nine. They lived next door to each other, and she loved nothing more than to follow him around. He was her first friend, and she eventually became his first and only love. (One night, back in 1948, Mickey had been drinking just enough to be nostalgic. Henry, "Big" Mike, and Francis had just finished a nice dinner with him and enjoyed hearing about the greatest love ever.) They had raised three kids, the two younger ones both died heroes during the winter months of '44, at the Battle of the Bulge. Mickey was devastated by their death, but proud as hell at how they fought tooth and nail with the Nazis. That was it for the Moore's, as far as Henry knew.

He picked up the phone and called "Big" Mike at work. "I assume you heard."

"I got a call. You alright?"

"I will be after I find out who killed him but not before."

"You think it was intentional? Some of the guys say it looks like a text book hit and run," Mike said, trying to be as delicate as he could.

It wasn't his strong suit. He did tough really well. He did loyal better than anyone. Sensitivity was a little foreign to Mike.

Henry knew this about him and appreciated his effort.

"It may sound a little thin, but it appears someone had been parked behind Mickey's car long enough to smoke almost a pack of cigarettes. They closed off the area within minutes, so I know the car didn't leave after the accident. I don't know if it left before… but, as Mickey used to say, 'There are no coincidences.'"

"You may be right. I'll head over to the 9th and check with the lads and see if they've found anything else out."

"Thanks, Mike. I appreciate the help…Mickey would've too."

"Mickey may not have been a cop, but everyone loved him. He was one of our own, and if you're right, and there is someone out there who waited for him, like a coward, and ran him down…we'll find the bastard." His voice had risen to a measured rage. Then he lowered it. "I'll help you with the arrangements. I'll call Francis and we can put together a wake that won't soon be forgotten."

"You are the best, Mike."

After he hung up the phone, Henry started to pace around the apartment. He thought about the man who had visited him.

"What was his name?" he said aloud.

The business card was still in his trousers. When Henry read the name "William H. Brown," it made him laugh. It was a short burst, and seemed out of place, but it happened. Henry didn't dwell on it.

The phone rang. "Hello?" he said.

"It's Luna, I just heard about your old friend, Mickey. I'm so sorry."

Hearing her voice through the line was a pleasant twist to his miserable day.

"You are very kind, Luna."

What he didn't add was that he missed her. It wasn't the sort of thing Henry would say, but he knew he did. Having her around for those few weeks, back in January, had been comfortable in a way he had never imagined.

"Mike told me he was going to talk to you about handling the wake. Though I didn't know Mickey, I want to help. I will call Sylvia, too. I hope it isn't too presumptuous, but we can handle the food. Is that okay, Henry?"

He could see the expression on her face in his mind. It was good to have friends.

"Mickey would've liked you. Give my thanks to Sylvia."

Henry continued pacing. His addled brain was starting to clear a bit. Having the wake handled was one less thing to worry about, and it seemed those gray cells had turned their attention to the notebook.

There was one note, "fishing anti Katherine," that seemed less confusing than the others. Henry remembered every time Mickey wanted to use the word "real" he substituted "fishing," as in a fishing reel. So he had actually written, "The real anti Katherine."

The most famous Katherine whom Henry could think of, was Catherine the Great. Could this be a reference to her? It was possible, as he was sure Mickey wasn't above misspelling her name. But what was the opposite of Catherine? Henry didn't have any idea, but he did have resources. Over the years, he had developed an encyclopedic knowledge of the references made available at the public library.

Henry grabbed his hat and coat, locked his door, and headed to the office. He was getting his second wind.

Chapter Ten

The Flatiron building on 23rd had housed his office since Tommy "The Knife" burned Henry out of the old place. It was a little bit bigger, had a better view, a few plants, and some filing cabinets. Henry had settled in and sat behind his desk. A pot of coffee was brewing, and the air was filled with the aroma of thinking.

Henry had gotten tired of flipping through to the back of Mickey's notebook. He carefully copied each of the three pages into his own notes. Next, he numbered them and turned his attention to page two. With his head clear from the shower, he started to consider the scribbling. There were the numbers one through six written down the side with each one having two words – which didn't make sense – and then squares or tiny stick figures. He took a deep breath and asked himself the question, "What is the first thing to come to mind?"

Before he could answer himself, he heard some short, stubby, and highly excitable steps coming down the hall. Henry knew the little patter of annoying feet.

He got up and went to meet Bobby at the door.

He waited for the knock, and then opened it.

"Hello, Bobby."

"Hello, Henry. I heard about your friend. I am sorry." He took a heavy breath.

This was strange for Bobby. Henry used to his frantic ramblings and his nauseating happiness, but to see him in such a solemn state was unsettling. Henry had grown to tolerate Bobby, and, seeing him now, he felt the slightest bit of fondness for the strange little man.

"Thanks...buddy."

Bobby flashed a brief smile.

"His death was not as it should have been. A man like that, after a life of helping people, didn't deserve for his days to end. But, sometimes the hands of time cannot be slowed or altered, even if we think we can change what might have been. Is there anything I can do to help? I am at your service."

Bobby never ceased to amaze Henry. In a flash, the tiny, annoying man had touched Henry. Then, a scant moment later, his mouth had spewed forth something philosophical and elegant. It didn't even sound like Bobby; the manner, tone, and vocabulary were all wrong. Words of condolence seldom had an effect on Henry, but this was different. It was, as if, it had come from someone else, perhaps someone from a different age entirely.

Henry didn't have time to add "The Mystery of Bobby" to his list of things to unravel, but maybe after Mickey's killer was found, he would give it some thought.

There was a silence as Henry considered Bobby's offer to help. It couldn't hurt, he thought. "Come on back...I want to show you something."

Bobby followed Henry into his office. Henry handed his notebook to him and said, "Mickey tended to write in code. I hadn't talked to him in a few years, and he always changed the way he took his notes. Back in the day, we used to have breakfast, and he would explain his latest method for encryption. I guess what I am asking is, what is the first thing that comes to mind when you see this?"

Bobby, excited again, said, "Oh, I love a puzzle! This page looks like a list. Not just a list. It looks like a list of names. Those two people with the stick figures have something in common, as do the three people with the picture frames."

"Picture frames..." Henry said aloud, then continued, "Those are not just squares...they are thicker. They do look like picture frames. Bobby, that is a good find!"

Bobby was nearly bursting with excitement. "What do you think the picture frames mean?"

"I think they represent art. Maybe those names are a list of painters?"

Bobby, almost hyperventilating, said, "Then the stick figures are statues. Those other people must be sculptors."

Henry smiled. "This is a good lead. I need to make some calls. Thanks for your help, buddy."

Bobby did a little leap, spun around, and bolted out of the office. He yelled as he exited the waiting room, "Any time, buddy!"

Henry had to smile. He took a dirty coffee mug, grabbed an even dirtier towel, and made a half-hearted attempt at wiping it out. After pouring a cup, he added some sugar and stirred it while he returned to his desk. In his left hand he held the coffee cup, and on the desk, the open notebook. The coffee tasted good, but the idea about painters and sculptors seemed a touch sour.

Why would Mickey get bumped off because he was looking into a bunch of artists?

Henry didn't think artists were the murdering type, but he couldn't be sure. Katarina knew much more about the art scene, so he jotted down a note to ask her what she thought about it.

Henry picked up the phone and called the public library. He asked the head librarian, Marian, if she had any books about Catherine the Great, especially ones that might have portraits that had been painted during her lifetime. She promised to find some and leave them behind the counter for him to pick up.

Henry flipped forward to page three and said aloud, "Anti Catherine."

Bobby's sense that the list had something to do with art, plus Mr. Brown being an art collector, seemed to be pointing in the same direction. Henry mulled this over for a few minutes and then he said to the walls, "Not artists, collectors!"

He flipped back to the list, grabbed a yellow pad, and counted the letters next to each number.

The sixth number had seven letters, followed by five letters. If this was "W-i-l-l-i-a-m B-r-o-w-n," then Henry would have a great start at cracking the code.

Chapter Eleven

November 10, 1902 was a date Henry knew well. It had very little significance, besides being on the cornerstone of his favorite building in New York.

Henry walked towards 5th and 42nd street. If New York was a jungle, then the kings of the jungle could be found guarding the Stephen A. Schwarzman Building. South of the main steps, surveying those who passed by seeking knowledge, was Patience. Always vigilant, Fortitude kept an eye open for trouble. They were originally called "Leo Astor" and "Leo Lenox," named for the founders of the New York Public Library, but Mayor LaGuardia renamed them in the 1930s, and it stuck.

Patience and Fortitude would both be required to find Mickey's killer. As Henry walked past, there were tourists gawking at Patience and speaking in a tongue he couldn't recognize. The words were unclear, but the admiration was evident.

Henry knew his way around the library and loved wandering the stacks, but today there wouldn't be any time for a bibliophile to explore.

Marian was helping an elderly man check out his books. Henry waited patiently in line. When she saw Henry, Marian reached under the counter and pulled out three books. The smile told

Henry he could grab them and go find a nook or cranny and dig in. Five minutes later, Henry was reading all about Catherine the Great.

Catherine took power when her husband, Peter III, was deposed in a conspiracy. This was all very interesting, but didn't seem relevant. A thought crossed Henry's mind. He knew so little about the list of names that it was hard to tell if any of the history of her life might be important. Still, there wasn't much else to do before meeting Katarina for dinner, so he continued for another two hours.

Henry's head was swimming with miscellaneous facts and bits of Russian history. His second wind was gone, and he yawned as he closed up the third book. He walked past a couple of NYU students who were more focused on studying one another than their physics. The young man had his hand on her elbow and was whispering something in the blonde's ear. She was giggling. It was nice.

The front desk was quiet now. Henry walked up and placed the books on the counter.

"Hello, Marian, how are you today?"

"Mr. Wood," she said in a quiet voice. "It is nice to see you today. Were the books helpful?"

"I enjoyed them, but I am not sure if I am on the right track."

There was a glint in her eye. "Are you working on a case?"

Henry knew she liked to live vicariously through his adventures. He didn't feel like telling her he was his own client doing a job that felt like an anvil on his chest.

"Yes, it is a case. A real puzzler."

"Oh, how exciting! May I ask how Catherine the Great is mixed up in your case?"

"I am not sure she is; it is just a hunch. It was something I read."

"A clue?" she said, hopeful, in a voice which was a bit too loud. If she hadn't been so excited, she might have shushed herself.

Henry held up one finger to his mouth, with a smile. Marian blushed and looked down at her feet.

Henry pulled his notebook out and flipped to the passage about Catherine. He slid it across the counter. Marian's blush faded as she picked it up. She tilted her head to one side and pulled a pencil out from the bun in her hair. She tapped it lightly on the counter, the wood end making a slight rapping noise.

She asked, "Are you sure it's spelled correctly?"

"I got the notes second hand, but Catherine is spelled the same as it was in the books."

"That isn't what I meant. Could it be 'Antikythera'?"

Henry wasn't sure what she had just said, but he didn't want to let on. So he fixed a pensive look on his face in the hope she might elaborate if he didn't respond right away.

"I don't know what 'Anti Catherine' means, but maybe the person didn't know how to spell 'Antikythera'?"

Henry decided to end his own suffering, even if it tarnished his image in Marian's eyes. "I think that is reasonable, as I don't know how to spell 'Anti...' In fact, I don't know how to say it, or what you are talking about."

Marian gave Henry a pat on the hand, "It's okay...not many people do. It is a fascinating story..."

A woman with books on gardening was now standing behind Henry. Marian gave her a smile and said, "I will be right with you." She looked back at Henry and continued, "...The story would take a little while to explain. Why don't I find some information about it for you? It's starting to get busy. Maybe you could come back tomorrow?"

Henry turned his head and said, "Sorry Miss," then smiled at Marian. "I will see you tomorrow."

He tipped his hat and walked towards the door. Heading out of the building, he had a good feeling about this "anti" thingy. He was anxious to learn what she was talking about...then he spied

Patience and decided that it was an omen, or, at the very least, some good advice.

He turned his thoughts to Katarina.

Chapter Twelve

Arthur's assumption of displeasure at the update had proven to be correct.

The staff hid while Arthur ate his breakfast, seemingly immune to the screaming from his employer. During the rant, a bone china tea cup and two vases had fallen victim to Garneau's rage. He circled the room yelling about incompetence, calling Arthur names and firing him…twice.

The breakfast rampage lasted for close to an hour. Garneau worked up such a lather, he needed another bath. The French maid and Claude, upon hearing the ruckus, had curtailed their amorous activities. Claude went to find shelter in the car. The maid went to fill the tub for Garneau. He soaked until the water was lukewarm, then he bellowed out a command for more warm water. The poor maid needed to make two return trips that morning.

"Hurricane Andre," as Arthur sometimes called him, though not to his face, lost steam after a while and was downgraded to a tropical storm. Even Andre knew that his bluster was gone. So he dressed again, ordered Claude to come around with the car, and told Arthur they were going to visit the Matisse place.

Claude knew the way to the gallery. When his boss needed to go someplace but didn't have anything important to do, he would go to the gallery at 41 East 57th Street, in the Fuller building. Pierre Matisse, a talented artist, who was born in the shadow of his father, Henri Matisse, opened the gallery in 1931. The gallery was the site of Andre's first legitimate art purchase, a piece by the surrealist, Paul Delvaux.

They arrived, and Claude waited in the car. For an hour, Andre Garneau and Pierre shared a glass of wine and talked about art. Then he returned to the car and instructed Claude to drive to the church.

The pieces of art, which Andre had purchased from legitimate gallery owners like Pierre, were nice, but they were just for show. The real treasures were locked in a secure room with perfect lighting, steady temperature, and a single velvet chair. He had three lost master works, which had disappeared during WWI, and two more which were presumed destroyed when the Germans rolled through Hungary. Knowing that people were searching for his treasures made owning them extra enjoyable.

There were others around the world, who like to admire their own ill-gotten art, in tiny rooms. This group's members knew of one another, but never met. A competitive club (some might say ruthless), but without each other, the game would be meaningless.

Like any good sport, there needed to be rules. One of the rules was that notice would be given before visiting the "other gallery,", as they referred to it.

It wasn't a gallery at all, but a cathedral, with a priest who was the intermediary.

Each member of this club had established a trigger location. They would go there first and stay an hour. This would give the local eyes and ears time to "announce" the pending visit. The priest would then become available for "confessions."

Andre Garneau had chosen Pierre Matisse's gallery for his trigger. It was the only place he could imagine spending an hour where he would not have looked out of place. He had considered choosing one of his favorite restaurants, but then he would have had to limit his visits.

This was not acceptable.

The thought had crossed his mind that he could choose a restaurant he did not like, but then he would have needed to endure an hour of dreadful dining, also a non-starter. He chose Pierre's gallery because it was logical.

The second rule was that the trigger location must not be "involved" in any way. Pierre was completely on the up and up, and would have objected had he known how he was being used. The semi-frequent purchases by Andre made Pierre's the perfect place for him to be seen. Even Claude didn't know that the gallery stop was associated with visits to the cathedral, because he had been driving Garneau there since long before it had become Andre's trigger.

Claude had noticed, however, that Garneau only seemed to go to confession after their visits to Pierre's place. He never understood why, but assumed that Garneau was getting the better of the young Matisse, and was feeling a need to repent.

Garneau walked up the steps. The inside was warm and comforting, but most of all, it was dark and quiet. He lit a candle, prayed, and then entered the confessional.

"Forgive me, Father, for I have sinned...."

A whisper answered him. "Yes, and you will again. Do be quick – I don't have all day...my son," the priest said in a mocking tone.

In truth, the priest was not actually ordained. He was, however, a great forger and had conned his way into the church. He was hiding from enemies. They were looking for him in Europe and even North Africa. A few people suggested he might have gone to America, but nobody suspected a Catholic church.

He was called Father Patrick Liguori...which wasn't his name at all. He was one of the greatest fences in the world. His success was so profound that he had to go into hiding and now only dealt in works, which nobody else would touch. Before an item made it to him, it would travel to dozens of countries, be passed through many careful hands, and eventually be made available in a private auction.

"I understand that someone hired a P.I. to try to find out who the collectors are?" Garneau asked.

This was news to Patrick, but he played it cool. "So what if they did? Why do you bother me with such matters?"

"I want to know who is poking around in my business. I want to know if it was you!"

"Your fatness is equaled only by your stupidity. I already know who all of you are. Idiot."

This stunned Andre, as he immediately realized the absurdity of his accusation. In his rage at breakfast, the first name to pop into his head was Patrick's. He hadn't thought it through, which was not at all like him.

"I am sorry…you are right." Apologies were also not like him, and it scratched his throat as he said it. "Do you know if it is one of the other collectors?"

"This is the first I am hearing about it." After a brief pause, Patrick decided not to be too hard on Andre. He was, after all, one of his best clients. "I do appreciate you bringing this to my attention. It's best that I take some precautions before the upcoming auction."

"Yes, I agree," Andre said eagerly. He wanted to ask about the auction, but knew better. The third rule was to never speak about the art, especially in the confessional. It had happened once: the next day, the gentleman's home was raided and his collection was seized by the authorities. That was the rumor, at least. Whether it was true or not, the thought was enough to keep everyone in line.

Andre said nothing more and returned to the car. He felt very much on edge. He needed to take action, and had believed that a visit to the church would make him feel better. It had not.

Chapter Thirteen

Hans had walked for a couple of hours. He had slept for a few. His apartment was clean, neat, and meticulously geometric. Along one wall of the living room, a China cabinet by Paul Frankl, with its slate gray base, and ivory doors, was precisely centered. His streamlined sofa, also by Frankl, was made from black lacquer and covered in black leather. There was a simple rectangular, black coffee table, art deco lamps and sconces, and a rug with a giant red circle in a field of gray and black overlapping rectangles.

His tiny office, a converted bedroom, had a desk by De Coene Freres with four simple drawers and tapered legs, also of black lacquer and sitting on nickel feet. Next to the desk was a Manik Bagh side table designed by Eckart Muthesius.

In short, he lived in a shrine to the years between the two wars. They were his happiest days, his youth, and though he grew up poor, he was too happy to notice. WWII ended his bliss.

Hans had showered, shaved, put on his dressing robe, and made a light breakfast, though it was well past noon. Two cups of coffee later, after having read the paper he picked up on the walk home, he washed the plate and silverware and put them away. He washed and dried the coffee cup and returned it to its place amongst the others, which never got used. He dressed in a tailored suit and picked out a tie with a small amount of blue in it. Before he left, he went to his desk, opened a journal, and wrote on a piece of note paper his tasks for the day. He handn't sat at the desk, but chose instead to stand, so as not to break the crease in his pants.

It took less than thirty minutes to walk to the Flatiron building. He climbed the steps and entered the hallway. Hans noted the numbers on the door, and he surmised that the office in question was at the far end of the hall. One door, on his right, opened slightly as he walked past. He gave a quick glance and saw a small man peering through the gap at him.

He was glad it wasn't this man that he was there to see.

The glass on the door read "Henry Wood Detective Agency". He tried the handle, but, it appeared to be locked. He looked at his pocket watch and noted that it was still business hours. Strange that there wasn't a secretary, at the very least, during the day.

Perhaps this Henry Wood isn't going to be up to the job, he thought.

He would give the detective fifteen minutes to return. He was quite prepared to go see the next detective on his list. The reputation of Mr. Wood was excellent, but Hans found this little inconvenience intolerable.

* * *

Henry noticed the man waiting outside his door as he strode down the hall.

I really need to get a girl to manage the office, he thought as he walked down the hall. For years he hadn't been able to afford to hire anyone, but that wasn't the case now. After years of saving, he was finally comfortable, and who knew how many clients he was losing while he was out on a case. Henry decided he would add it to his list, and give it priority, especially since he was sure that his current case would be keeping him busy.

Henry had no idea how long the man had been waiting. Bobby popped out of his office and walked towards the stairs. As he passed by Henry, Bobby whispered, "He has been there for about ten minutes. I don't trust him."

Henry didn't say anything, but tipped his hat towards Bobby, in lieu of a "thanks".

"Hello, sir! I apologize for the inconvenience. I had to step out briefly." Henry opened the door and showed the man inside.

"My name is Hans. I'm looking for someone with your skills to do some...research."

"That sounds like something for a grad student. What type of research?" Henry motioned for him to follow him into his office and offered to make some coffee. Hans declined.

Hans took a seat, when offered, and then asked if he could smoke. Henry nodded and held up a lighter. Hans offered one of his imported cigarettes to Henry, which he accepted.

Hans said, "You would not be working for me directly, but for my employer. He prefers anonymity, though you will meet him, if your services prove to be right for the job."

Henry listened and smoked.

"My employer is a very wealthy man who enjoys the finer things in life. A piece of art, or more aptly, a piece of history, is going to be made available for sale, and he is interested in buying it."

"That is interesting: he collects art. Where do I come in?"

"If we decide to hire you, we will require you to look into the seller and the item. It will be very expensive and caution must be taken. My employer does not wish to purchase a fake."

"I can find out anything you want to know about a person, but what makes you think I am qualified to authenticate art? I'm not an art historian. Surely there are men more qualified than me to determine the authenticity of some old painting?"

"The object is not a painting...but that isn't important. What is of concern to my employer is that the object actually exists. We only require that you learn a little about the seller and verify that the object is as described. If it is determined that this object does exist, and my employer wishes to participate in the sale, he will be given an opportunity to have an expert authenticate the piece."

"Who is the seller?" Henry took out his notebook and prepared to take notes.

Hans took a long drag on the cigarette. "I am not ready to hire you, Mr. Wood. I have a few questions, if you don't mind?"

Henry closed the notebook, leaned back in his chair, "I don't mind at all. Fire away."

"How long have you been a private detective?"

"Almost thirteen years."

Hans had known the answer, but wanted to see if Henry would exaggerate.

"Would you be able to commit to my employer with 100% of your time?"

Henry didn't have any other clients, nor did he want to be distracted from finding Mickey's killer, but his gut told him that Hans' employer might be on Mickey's list.

"I just finished up a case. I was going to take some time off, but I could handle this job first."

"That is excellent. My employer is prepared to pay $10,000, plus daily expenses. He would require complete discretion. Do you work alone?"

Henry was quick on his feet. He knew that if this guy was involved in the case Mickey was working on, then he would need some help. "I have a couple of people who work with me, beating the bushes as it were. They can keep a secret, if that's what you mean."

Hans thought for a moment. He had expected that this was a one-man shop. "I would need to meet your associates before I make a decision."

Henry hadn't counted on this request. He bluffed.

"No problem...they'll both be back in town day after tomorrow."

Hans thought about this. He had decided that Henry was the man for the job and really didn't want to wait. "I prefer to get started, as soon as possible... but I suppose one extra day will be fine. My employer is cautious, as I said, so shall we say noon?"

Henry set his cigarette in the ash tray, stood and extended his hand. "I will see you then."

Chapter Fourteen

The icy cold shower seemed like a necessity.
Who killed Mickey? What had caused Katarina to show up after so many years? Had Marion changed her hair?
After an hour of getting ready, which was about thirty minutes longer than usual, Henry decided enough was enough. Slowly, his focus turned to the woman who haunted his dreams.
He reminded himself that she was just a friend. He had never told her how he felt; she would be expecting to dine with her buddy, not the lovesick guy who had followed her around like a puppy so many years before. He wasn't sure if he could even remember what being "lovesick" felt like anymore. Years of hardening his heart had made him immune to such foolishness, or at least…he hoped he was immune. Luna had tested his resolve not too long ago…
He imagined how the upcoming dinner might go as he sat at the kitchen table. Henry had left plenty of time, even with his extra fussing over the tie choice. He considered rereading her letters, but thought better of it. The best course of action, he thought, was to let her do most of the talking.
He had a plan.
Henry hailed a cab. It wasn't terribly far to the restaurant, but he

was running on only a couple of hours sleep, and he had already done his fair share of walking today, so it didn't seem unreasonable.

He arrived fifteen minutes early, which would be thirty minutes before Katarina showed up "fashionably late." Henry took a seat at the bar and ordered a beer.

There were four Wall Street bankers smoking cigars at the far end of the bar. At a table nearby, two bubbly stewardesses were enjoying some drinks and batting their eyes at the bankers. About half of the tables were full. The waiters glided around the tables. It was much like Henry remembered, though he imagined it would have been busier. He considered how long it had been since his last visit. All those years ago… perhaps the steady crowd of diners had started to drop off. He decided to ask.

"Hey buddy, it seems a little slow tonight."

The bartender, who was setting out some new martini glasses, looked up. "Yes, it is. But, it'll pick up in an hour or so."

"I haven't been here in a few years. You still have the best steaks in town?"

"Yes, we do, sir," he said with pride. "They are so tender that they melt in your mouth. Some say that when they take that first bite, they get a glimpse of heaven."

Henry's mouth began to water.

The bankers and the stewardesses had moved to a larger table, gotten some more drinks, and been joined by two more stunning blonds. There was a lot of giggling from the ladies and winking from the guys.

No mystery there, Henry thought. While he nursed his beer, Henry resisted the urge to snap his head around each time the door opened. Instead, he found a good reflection of the front door in the bar mirror and kept his eyes peeled for her arrival.

When it was finally Katarina who walked through the door in a brilliant blue coat, it seemed that time slowed. He stopped staring and took a sip of beer.

He felt a light touch on his shoulder. "Henry Wood..."

A coolness came over him. He was confident and surefooted. This had never happened before, when she was around.

He stood up and gave her a light hug, more polite than anything. She hugged back with a moderately tight squeeze. They lingered, and then parted.

A waiter was waiting to show them to their table. Henry helped her off with her coat and handed it to someone nearby, who may or may not have worked at the restaurant.

Her dress was black and curvy. Henry couldn't help but say, "You look beautiful. The years have not only been kind...they have been complimentary."

"Seeing you, makes the years melt away. It seems like just yesterday, we were at that diner."

Henry pulled out the chair for her and then took his own. A man lit the candle on their table and asked if they wanted anything to drink. Katarina ordered two martinis, the same way she had ordered them the last time they were there together. Henry wasn't sure, but he thought she might have been wearing the same earrings.

"Those were some good years," he said, feeling that old familiar warmth.

Katarina reached out and took his hand. "My dear Henry, I did miss you." She smiled, then let go of his hand when another waiter stopped with a pitcher of water. "It was a hard decision, leaving New York, but I had to. You know that."

"What have you been up to over the last decade or so?"

"I went to visit my aunt in Wyoming after I got the news. I spent a couple of years losing myself in books. And then I got a message...that Paul was alive, hiding in Egypt."

There it was...that old kick in the gut. He knew it well, it came to him each time she talked about her fiancé Paul. He had disappeared and been listed as missing in action. Henry had tried to console Katarina, but she was in denial, and decided she needed a change. Henry had always thought she would be back. When the record turned up eighteen months ago, he was sure she had returned, but when it was followed up with nothingness, the wound was opened, again.

He decided not to mention the record.

She took a sip of water, giving Henry a chance to speak.

He chose not to take it.

"I joined him in Cairo and found work in a gallery. You know how I love art."

There it was again: art.

"Yes, I do." Henry could see her ring finger was bare, without breaking eye contact. "So you married Paul, like you had planned?"

She shrugged. "Well, no, we hadn't known each other very long before he proposed. The war, life, and his own stupidity, took the luster away. We spent two years together in Cairo and then I moved on."

Henry knew the emotions creeping up on him had been buried for many years. It was unsettling to have them surface and possibly, dangerous.

She took his hand again and looked into his eyes. "I should have stayed in New York – with you."

Henry mustered a practiced confident, charming smile. He stared into her eyes with such depth that the rest of the restaurant seemed to fade away.

He didn't even notice the priest eating alone in the corner, or that he seemed to be watching them.

Chapter Fifteen

Dr. Schaeffer and Hans had been enjoying some maultasche, a traditional Swabian dish made with an outer layer of pasta dough and filled with minced meat, a bit of smoked meat, bread crumbs, and onions. They look similar to Italian ravioli, but to Dr. Schaeffer, they were a reminder of his nanny's cooking when he was a boy.

The conversation was sparse, as both men were enjoying their meal, the beer, and Wagner playing in the background. They preferred to savor the food. The talk would come later.

To most people, the knock at the door would have gone unnoticed with Der Filegende Hollander playing, but the exceptional ears of Dr. Schaeffer heard the three taps clearly. Soft feet treaded down the hallway, the door opened, and an envelope was handed to the woman. She said nothing, giving only a nod. The woman walked to the dining room and cleared her throat.

"Herr Doctor, a message."

He motioned her over and received the envelope. "Ick danke Ihnen". He didn't read it.

"Hans, how was your day, my friend?"

"It was productive. I selected three possible candidates, though I must admit, even the most highly regarded one has an air of seediness about him. If there were more time, I might reject them all, but as it stands, Mr. Henry Wood seems our best choice. I am to meet his associates at noon, day after tomorrow."

"Did he strike you as the sort who can keep a secret?"

"Yes, I believe he can. I am going to reserve final judgment until after the meeting. Tomorrow, I will visit the other two candidates, as neither was available today."

"That is excellent, Hans. I'm quite pleased. Now, let's see what the padre has to say." Dr. Schaeffer stood up and went to the sideboard, opened the top drawer, and removed a silver letter opener. With surgical precision, he sliced the envelope open. Removing the letter, he sat back down. From his jacket pocket, he retrieved his reading glasses, set them on his nose, and began to read aloud.

Doctor,

This letter is a courtesy. There is a rumor that someone is looking into the people interested in the wares I offer. Anonymity is of the utmost concern for all of my clients, so I felt obligated to make you aware of this situation. The upcoming auction date has not been set. I am inclined to put it on ice until this is resolved. I will not tolerate anyone messing about in my, or my clients', affairs.

Sincerely,

The Curator

Dr. Schaeffer returned the letter to the envelope. "This is an interesting turn. I wonder who might have..." He faded off at the end. A brief silence followed.

"Shall I keep our meeting with Mr. Wood?"

There was another long silence. Dr. Schaeffer, standing up,

walked slowly around the room, thinking. The needle on the Wagner was lifted. He bit the tip off of a cigar, lit it, and continued to pace back and forth.

Hans knew his routine and sat quietly, drinking his beer. The next move would come to his boss shortly.

"I believe you should," Dr Schaeffer said and added, "If the meeting goes well, pay him the retainer, and explain that he will be receiving further instructions at a later date, but to be ready at a moment's notice."

"Very good. Are there any other tasks for me?"

"Not right now, my friend. Do you have time for a game of chess?"

"I do, if you let me play white, and agree not to play the French Defense. I'm tired of losing to that opening."

"Agreed. I shall start with c4."

They played the first eight moves verbally while they walked to the study. Hans then considered whether he should try something new. He chose bishop to c4, not knowing if the doctor knew the variation.

Across the city, envelopes were being delivered to four other homes and one hotel.

Chapter Sixteen

Father Patrick enjoyed his sea bass, and indulged his sweet tooth with a piece of cheesecake. He sipped coffee for a while after his meal, left a generous tip, and then parted, grabbing a cab to a building where three of his more elderly parishioners lived.

Rose Webber, seventy-two and widowed, lived on the fifth floor and baked cookies, daily. She would often bring them down to the church, and for this, Patrick would visit her and play cribbage at least once per week. Her husband had been a hard worker his whole life, saved his pennies, and invested in Coca Cola stock when he and Rose were young. Eventually, he was able to retire and buy her the beautiful home she had always wanted.

On the third floor, Ginny and Doug, both seventy-five, lived among their collection of china that they had bought over a lifetime. Patrick liked visiting them, and even salivated over a few of the majolica pieces, which dated to 14th century Italy. If he had met them fifteen years ago, he would have robbed them blind – now they were just bobbles. Plus, he liked them both.

Patrick considered this affection for Rose, Ginny, and Doug as a personal character flaw. He assumed he must be getting old. They served their purpose, though.

It was not uncommon for Father Patrick to visit them, usually early in the morning or later in the evening. Everyone knew his face and was not at all surprised to see him in the halls. He never took the elevator, as he told everyone the exercise was good for spirit and body. In truth, Patrick hated taking the stairs, but it was a small sacrifice to maintain believability.

Unit 429, on the fourth floor, right next to the stairwell, was owned by a man nobody knew. The name on the box wasn't familiar to the residents. Everyone assumed the occupant just liked to keep to himself. The name, actually another alias for Father Patrick, wasn't known this side of the Atlantic. Whenever Patrick needed to tear off his collar and just have a nice cup of tea, as himself, he would simply pay a visit to Rose on floor five and then sneak back downstairs into his apartment.

The other priests were not surprised when Father Patrick didn't return, as he was known to stay out late… trying to find and help the homeless. Tonight, he stopped in to see Rose, knowing she would be out playing canasta. He knocked a couple of times, for show, then snuck into his own apartment.

The walls were adorned with paintings by Edgar Degas, Honoré Daumier, George Bellows, and Thomas Cole. Each was a copy, meticulously recreated by Patrick. At one point or another, he had possessed the originals, but then they were passed along. He didn't care much about owning originals, as his own copies meant far more to him, and his focus was on getting the big score. With each successful auction, he would crave one bigger and better, always telling himself he needed just one more to retire. Patrick had visions of living in the south of France and painting away the days.

Patrick sat down at his easel. He was working on an original piece. He could copy the masters, but somehow was unable to come up with his own ideas. He thought about the message he had received from that vile pig, Andre. He thought about his note and wondered if he had made the correct play. He was curious how the various collectors would react to his threat to delay the auction. He smiled. Patrick liked having these suckers, who were dying to give up their millions just to get a piece of history. He suspected that if any one of them tried to tell his forgeries from the real ones, there wasn't but one among them who could spot the difference.

He thought about The Falcon. He wondered what this bird of prey's reaction might be to his threat.

Tomorrow would be a busy day. He had plans to double check. In two days, the package would arrive, God willing, and he would need to make arrangements for individual viewings. Each prospective bidder would be taken to a different location. They would be allowed to spend up to two hours carefully examining the piece, and each would be permitted to bring an expert. Patrick laughed at this last rule, as his clients were much too vain to bring an expert, and thus cast their own "credentials" into question. To arrange separate viewings, Patrick had assembled individual teams. This was expensive, as the members of each team didn't know one another.

Over the years, Patrick had mastered living in the shadows. If forging was his best skill, reading people was a close second. He knew how to press buttons. Each team had been carefully built. Patrick could tell who might betray him and who would be loyal. He knew what motivated his prospects: to some he provided money, to others fear, and, to a few, friendship. Whatever it took to get people to do his bidding – and never speak of it – he did.

In his early years, before the war, he had pulled off some brilliant cons and was never caught. There were a couple of close calls, but he always had an out. During the war, however, he really flourished. There were all sorts of people stealing, selling, and dying. He excelled at profiting from the chaos. Working both sides of the street taught him the value of anonymity. By the time the shooting had stopped, he was wealthy beyond most people's wildest dreams. He was also a ghost.

It was then that he moved to the U.S. He spent years building up the network of people he would need to start fencing the works of art, which nobody else could touch.

He added a touch of yellow, then put his brush down and walked to the table in the center of the room. The plan sat patiently, waiting for at least one more review. His love of planning was perhaps his third greatest asset. Tonight he would review every detail. At 3:00 a.m., he would go to bed, confident in his vision and his plan.

Chapter Seventeen

Henry put Katarina in a cab around 10:30 p.m. and walked home. He tried to think about the case. He wanted to concentrate on Mickey…but the thoughts of her hauntingly beautiful eyes and soft touch were filling his head.

Mostly, they had spent the evening eating and drinking. The conversation was of the "good ole days." Henry had tried to ask her about what she was up to, why she was in town. He couldn't remember her giving him a straight answer.

Was she being evasive on purpose, or just letting the wine go to her head? She had mentioned working with art once or twice, and that she was in town on business. He thought she had said she would only be around for a few weeks, but he also remembered her mentioning that she was considering staying.

The only thing he was completely sure of: the steak was fantastic.

As Henry tossed his keys on the dresser, he gave a glance at the clock on the nightstand. It was 10:47. He grabbed a glass. The clink, clink, clink of the ice cubes and the fizz of the Coke were like the round bell going off. He had taken some time off, but the fight was back on, and it was time to focus on finding Mickey's killer.

He picked up the phone and dialed. When he heard the voice on the other end say "hello," he started.

"Mike, any news?"

"Nothing yet, Henry. We found an abandoned car...it was towed to the garage with some marks that might match the ones on Mickey's. I'll know tomorrow. The car itself appears to be wiped clean, and the registration is to an elderly woman in Poughkeepsie. She is in her 80s, and didn't know her car was missing. How about you?"

"I made a little headway, but not much. Well, I had a guy, possibly chiseled from granite, stop in today, looking to hire a private dick. He said he was shopping around, but I'm not sure he was being straight with me. He wouldn't let on much about the job, but it sounds like a pretty big payday. Too big a payday."

"Nothing wrong with making a living, buddy."

"I know, but something doesn't feel right. Look, I need a favor. It's a big one."

Mike had been back at work for about a month, but had so far been mostly chained to his desk. Still, Henry wasn't sure if he would go for it.

"Anything you need, it's yours."

"You still got some vacation time left?" Henry asked, already feeling guilty.

"Heck, yeah. I had a pile of sick leave, and even with everything going on, I still have a bunch. I didn't have to use any sick leave when I was out of commission, so I figure I have about six months worth."

Henry chuckled. "You ever taken a vacation?"

"Yeah, I went fishing once. Didn't catch anything but a cold."

"This is the deal. I may have implied to this guy that I have a few other people working here. My gut tells me that this new client may have been part of whatever Mickey was looking into. I can't say for sure, but I could use some backup. You mind taking a week or two off, and doing some moonlighting at Henry Wood Detective Agency?"

"You got it buddy – no charge," Mike said.

"I appreciate the gesture," Henry countered, "but this has got to be on the up and up. I am putting you on the payroll, and will let the client know you are on loan from the force. I may have implied that we've worked together before, too."

"Well, technically, we have worked together before. I was just getting paid by the city." Mike chuckled.

"Good point, my friend. One more thing: I think I need a secretary. If you have any ideas, let me know."

"I can't think of anyone, but I'll keep my eyes open. When do you need me?"

"I realize it is short notice, but if you could make it in by 11:00 day after tomorrow, the client is coming in at noon."

"I have the next two days off anyway, so no problem. I'll go down to the station and put in for the time off, then be at your place by 11:00."

"Thanks." Henry pushed the plunger down on the phone; as soon as he had a dial tone again, he got the operator to dial an old friend.

"Hello, this is Dr. Brookert."

Henry loved his old friend's phone etiquette. "Dr. Brookert, it's Henry Wood. I hope I haven't called too late."

"Don't be ridiculous, my dear boy. I am just reading some interesting Latin text about...well...I find it interesting, but I digress. What can I do for New York's best detective?"

"I am working on something now. It feels like it may be right up your alley, and I could really use your help."

The life of a NYU professor is not as thrilling as one might imagine. Henry and the professor met many years ago, at the library. Henry had been fascinated by a pile of old-looking books, and they had struck up a conversation, found that they got along well, and that each was interested in the other's career choices.

The idea of working on a case with Henry thrilled the usually understated professor. His voice was like a child's for the briefest of moments. He paused, regained his composure and then said, "It would be my great pleasure. I am at your service."

"I appreciate it. I intend to put you on the payroll, but it shouldn't interfere with your classes. Mostly, I will want to use your vast knowledge of art and the art world."

"It sounds like a very interesting case. When do I start?"

"Is there any chance you could be at my office day after tomorrow, in the morning around 11:00, for a few hours? If you have a class, it's okay. This is short notice."

"I have a class at 9:00 and then again at 3:00. I will see you at 11:00. Hey, I heard your place burned down a few months back. Did you get it cleaned up?"

"Oh, no, I got a new office in the Flatiron building."

"Great, I will see you then…Boss." "

Henry laughed. He was quite sure that the impression the professor had of the life of a detective was more glamorous than was actually the case. He hoped he wouldn't be too disappointed.

"I will not have you calling me 'boss.' Oh, and one more thing: I am looking to hire a full-time secretary. You know anyone who might be interested?"

"I don't, but I will ask around. When do you need her?"

"In truth, about three years ago, if I am being honest with myself."

Henry could almost hear the smile over the phone. "See you later."

Chapter Eighteen

The waves, cold, relentless, and seemingly unprovoked, had followed them since the day after they left the Tyrrhenian Sea. The crew and captain couldn't remember a longer, more miserable trip. To a man, they were a new crew; the captain had only been aboard since the year before, when The Siena left Yard 136 in Denmark. The Siena was a beautiful ship, her displacement 15,295 tons, the length overall or LOA stretching an impressive 491 feet, and the beam 64 feet. She had a top speed of 16.75 knots, but today, she was tired and worn, along with her crew and captain, and two Greek passengers.

Cargo ships sometimes have a handful of passengers, but not often. On this voyage, some palms were greased, so that two middle-aged, but muscular men could accompany a box. The manifest was clear, detailing every item aboard…except the box. For this courtesy, a whole bucket of grease was required. The captain didn't know the contents, nor did he care. The Greek men, who had guarded it for years, had a vague understanding of the contents. They knew some stories. They knew the people who had found it.

In their youth, they had both loved listening to the theories about what it was, that it might be cursed, and the speculation of hidden powers. Neither man had ever witnessed anything unusual from the object; it just looked like a box with gears, all shinny and impressive. It was a very old box. Both men now believed in the curse and, since they couldn't eat for all of the sea sickness, spent their days praying to Saint Nicholas, the patron saint of sailors, merchants, archers, thieves, and children. When this didn't work, they turned their attention to Saint Christopher, since they were traveling.

Today, the North Atlantic was rougher than any of the previous days. The captain didn't think they weren't in mortal danger, but that might have been hubris on his part. The year before, The Southern Districts, a former naval ship with a full load of bulk sulfur heading for Bucksport, Maine, had moved through gusts of force 9 squalls, and then force 8 gusts. On December 11, it was reported that they were overdue, and the search began.

The captain thought about his friend who had been a first mate on The Southern Districts. He wondered if the wreck would ever be discovered. His own first mate gave an update: force 9 winds, and squalls. There wasn't any sign of it letting up either.

The captain said a prayer.

The Siena would be lost at sea, though not on this day, or the next one, either.

Chapter Nineteen

The sleep was not the least bit restful. Henry had expected to dream of Katarina or to have nightmares about Mickey. Instead, he had short dreams. All night, he was chased or drowning or fighting with some strange man. Each mini drama had one thread of similarity: something beyond his control was causing pain, and his struggling against the control just made it worse.

Henry didn't like it. He preferred to be in control, even when asleep. Henry often remembered his dreams; he was also good at being lucid in the nocturnal stories. Last night, he was not, and it started his day off on the wrong foot.

When Henry got out of bed and walked to the bathroom, he hit his toe. It hurt, and it was bewildering to him. He had never hurt himself in his own home, even when drunk. After a short burst of cursing, which he generally didn't do, there wasn't any improvement in his toe. His gut told him that he should be careful today. It also told him that a big breakfast was in order, though, admittedly, his gut told him this on most mornings, and sometimes late at night.

Henry showered, shaved, clipped his toe nails, and spent several minutes looking at his big toe, which seemed none too pleased with him. Henry rewarded his disgruntled toe and all the other toes with a fresh pair of socks, never worn. This went a long way towards forgiveness.

He spent the first hour of the morning mostly lost in the trivial. It was as if the last 28 hours had so worn his brain, it needed some alone time. Henry let his mind wander aimlessly while his hands made a three egg omelet, brewed some coffee, buttered some toast, and then decided to add a bonus piece of toast, with grape jelly.

The radio gave some good news about a missing boy who had been found. A different man's voice talked about the weather and a violent storm in the Atlantic. Henry noted the weather report and gave a look to the corner to see if his umbrella was there. It was, and ready for action. Henry changed the station and listened to some music, a tune by Stan Kenton, "The Peanut Vendor", which always reminded him of baseball. Henry thought about Vero Beach, which is where his beloved Brooklyn Dodgers had been holding spring training since 1949. This led his brain conveniently back to Mickey.

Mickey was at the game, September 9, 1948, when Rex Barney threw a no-hitter, having chosen to skip an afternoon of stalking some hysterical woman's husband who was cheating on her with an even more hysterical typing clerk. Henry couldn't remember what happened with that case, but he remembered Mickey feeling genuinely bad that he hadn't invited Henry to come along. Mickey liked to play pranks, tease, and give him a hard time, but he knew that the Dodgers were sacred; if he had known it would be an historical game, he would have gladly taken the stakeout duty so that Henry could go. Henry knew this because Mickey had told him about 1,000 times.

Almost two years later, on August 31, 1950, Mickey got a feeling. He had been planning to go to the track that day, and had given Henry the day off. There hadn't been much work. Henry remembered that was about the time he started to think about going out on his own. Mickey called a friend and got two tickets down the first base line. Then he called Henry and said they were going to the game. They had been to games before and seen some good ones, but nothing like the no-hitter. Henry remembered what his friend had said on the phone: "Henry, I know I gave you the day off, but we are going to Ebbets…I have a feeling". In truth, Mickey had said similar things before, and was usually wrong, but Henry didn't care. He would never turn down a chance to see the Dodgers play.

Only one Brooklyn Dodger in history has ever hit four home runs. He was kind enough to do it for Henry on that last day of August. Or at least, that is how Henry liked to remember it.

He got up from the kitchen table, turned off the radio, and went to his dresser in the bedroom. He opened the bottom drawer and pulled out a stack of magazines. In the middle of them, perfectly flat, in perfect condition, was the scorecard from that day. He read through every batter. It was as if he was back at Ebbets with his friend and mentor.

He put it away. Henry pulled out his notebook, dated the first clean page, and made a list for the day. His mind seemed clearer now and it was time to get back on the case.

Chapter Twenty

He listened for any shuffling around inside, as he walked past Bobby's office; he slowed up a bit. Henry wasn't interested in one of Bobby's long stories and was sure that if Bobby heard him in the hall, he would be knee deep in a lengthy tale, before he knew what hit him. He checked his watch. Nine o'clock and time to get back to work on Mickey's case. The empty receptionist desk suddenly bothered Henry. Had he really been doing everything Mickey had taught him? He sat down at the empty desk to think.

Thirty minutes passed and he still didn't know why he had never bothered to hire someone. There were countless times it would have been handy. How many clients had he lost because they showed up while he was out? It didn't look professional.

The thought crossed his mind that he might not be good enough to catch Mickey's killer. The doubt washed over him like a cold northerly wind, and it chilled him to the bone. Mickey had wandered into his life at just the right moment, but now he wasn't sure if he had spent enough time learning the ropes. His old boss was always testing him. Henry had loved it.

Could this be the final exam? Henry pushed aside the sick feeling he remembered from school. This test he couldn't bluff his way through.

Footsteps were coming down the hall; Henry hopped to his feet and went to the door. He heard a knocking, but it was a few doors down. He heard voices greeting each other and a door being closed. Henry walked back into his office and made some coffee. The view out the window didn't provide any inspiration, but he looked anyway.

When you are stuck, make a list, he thought, echoing the words of his mentor.

He flipped open his notebook and set it on the desk. The pencil was dull, so he sharpened it. First item...

The fears were strangling his mind. The blank page staring back at him screamed a deafening rebuke. *What do you do next? First item, who are the players in the New York art scene?* Just getting it on paper was a start, but the fears were coming faster than the ideas.

He opened the desk drawer. There was the card for Mr. Brown, who might or might not be wearing a brown suit today. It was the only item on his list, but maybe if he started at the top of the (very short) list, he may find a few more items to add.

Henry locked the office door and headed out to pay Mr. Brown a visit.

The metaphorical wind, which had chilled him earlier, was replaced by a very real arctic blast in Henry's face. His hat nearly got away from him, but his reflexes were still sharp. Hat in one hand, he used the other to hail a cab. The driver knew the address, and Henry was thankful he wasn't chatty.

Traffic in Manhattan was brutal, but they got there. Henry paid him and, with one hand on his fedora, exited the cab.

Mr. Brown's secretary was a stunning brunette. She politely asked Henry to take a seat and then informed Mr. Brown that he was waiting. A few minutes later the office door opened, and Mr. Brown, wearing a different brown suit, invited Henry in and offered him a chair.

"Mr. Wood, how may I help you today?"

"I don't want to take a lot of your time; I know you are busy. When we met the other day, I was unprepared, and for that, I am sorry." Henry had decided on the ride over to come clean about Mickey being dead.

"I'm happy to help and I do appreciate your being brief, as I have a meeting in about ten minutes."

"I'll get to the point, then. I don't know why Mickey wanted to talk to you, not completely. He was killed yesterday, and I am not sure it was an accident. I used to work for him, and he means a lot to me, so I was in his office looking for something which might help me find his killer." Henry paused when the secretary popped her head in and reminded Mr. Brown of his meeting.

"I'm sorry to hear it. Were you able to figure out why he wanted to see me?"

"I found some notes...it appears he was working on a case involving art. I was wondering if you might recognize any of these names." Henry took out his notebook.

"I might, as I do know most of the best collectors in New York. I am quite proud of my own collection."

Henry wasn't sure why he didn't read the list in order, but he didn't. Mr. Brown's reaction to the first two names was a simple shrug and a shake of the head. "I don't have a first name, but it seems there is a Dr. Schaefer," Henry said.

"Yes, he is a well known collector. I have seen him at gallery openings, though I couldn't say that I know him. We have even gone after a few of the same items at Sotheby's."

"Did you win the bids?"

"I have won some, but regardless of whether I win or lose, I always suspect that he has gotten the better of me. I don't like to admit it, but he has a sharp eye."

"What about the name Andre Garneau?"

The moment that Mr. Brown heard the name, he sat up in his chair. "He is a pig! That bastard wouldn't know a Rodin from a rodent. Nobody knows where his money comes from, but if I were to guess, I would say he has stolen it. He doesn't love art – he loves attention. His appetite for art is almost as great as his appetite for food. I would not call him a collector. He is more of a hoarder."

Henry noted the strong reaction and the comments. He read the other names, but Mr. Brown didn't seem to know any of the last few.

"I have just one more question," Henry said, "are you familiar with an object called the 'Antikythera Mechanism'?"

Mr. Brown was motionless, unnaturally so, for the briefest of moments. His eyes didn't blink, but Henry saw his pupils change.

"No, I can't say I am familiar with it. Doesn't really sound like my cup of tea, some antique machine... no not at all. I am interested in traditional art, paintings, sometimes sculptures, but never something so pedestrian. I haven't heard of it at all. What is it?"

The length of the answer was as telling as the pupils. Henry stood up and thanked Mr. Brown.

Chapter Twenty-One

Damn, Henry thought. Another person was waiting at his door while he was out. When he got closer, the collar made it even worse. Henry wasn't a religious man, but he respected those who were, and believed that they deserved to be treated well. *I really need a secretary.*

"Father, I am so sorry to have kept you waiting," Henry said as he unlocked the door.

"No matter, my son, a wee bit of time for quiet reflection is always appreciated."

Henry nodded and led the father in to the outer office. "May I take your coat?"

"Thank you."

Henry hung the priest's coat on the coat tree, then added his beside it. He led him into his office and asked, "Would you like a cup of coffee, Father?"

"No, that is quite alright."

"How may I help you?"

"I should probably begin by introducing myself. I am Father Patrick."

"Pleased to meet you, Father Patrick," Henry said, shaking his hand.

"I am with Saint Peter's over on Barclay. I heard about the loss of your friend, Michael Thomas Moore. I am deeply sorry for your loss. You have my condolences. I didn't know him well..." (he lied, as he didn't know him at all) "...but he was a good man. Is there anything I can do for you in this hour of need?"

Henry was a little surprised to be hearing from a priest about Mickey, as his friend had never been religious either. Of course, he knew Mickey was Catholic. Henry remembered that Mickey would attend mass on the major holidays and two or three times a year, when he was feeling extra full of sin, but it still seemed strange to have the priest calling. Henry couldn't recall Mickey ever mentioning St. Peter's, or any church for that matter, but the father seemed sincere.

"Father, we are planning the wake, and, to be honest, I didn't know where he attended mass. It has been a real shock."

"I know, it always is when one parts this earth, before his time. He wasn't a regular by any means, but he did stop in from time to time. It has been a while since we talked. He will be missed. Forgive me for asking, but I just heard of his passing this morning...how did he die? I wasn't aware of him being sick." Father Patrick was reading Henry and could tell that he had best keep it vague. He was also covering for his slight verbal blunder, though he didn't think Henry had noticed.

Henry, though not religious, was feeling the need to unburden himself. Father Patrick's question nudged Henry forward enough to get him to divulge his suspicions about Mickey's death. "Father, I don't think it was an accident. I think he was murdered."

Father Patrick lowered his head and said a prayer. Henry lowered his head, too.

"I didn't know Michael well enough to know about his family. He didn't mention anyone. Will you need help with the arrangements?"

Henry felt slightly better. The offer of help with the

81

arrangements was a Godsend. Henry explained to the priest that Mike and Luna were putting together the wake…and then he ran out of steam. The thought of burying his friend before he found the killer, or even working on the funeral, was almost more than he could bear. There was a long silence.

"Yes, Father, I would like some help with the arrangements. Let me talk to Luna and Mike. We will call you tomorrow. Your timing couldn't be better."

Father Patrick smiled. "I hope you are wrong about it being murder. I will pray that you find the truth, and if it is as you suspect, then I will pray you find the men who did it."

Henry shook the priest's hand and showed him to the door. He returned to his desk and opened his notebook. He started to write down his memory of the conversation, mostly out of habit, but partly because his gut told him it might be important. He jotted down that the priest was a few years older than him, possibly even early 50s, had blue eyes, and stood about 6 feet tall. He noted their conversation, the subject, the date, and then he paused. Something was bothering him.

Henry picked up the phone and dialed.

"Luna, Henry here."

"I know. How are you doing?" she said with a gentleness that Henry sorely needed.

"I'm doing fine. Thanks." And though he was not doing fine, hearing Luna's voice did make things better. "I was wondering if you and Mike had contacted a church yet?"

"No, we weren't sure where he went. Mike was going to call you later today and ask."

"I just had a visit from a priest, Father Patrick, who said he knew Mickey. He offered to help with the arrangements."

"That was very kind of him."

"Yes, it was." Henry said in a tone which had just a hint of accusation.

Luna picked up on it. "What is it Henry?"

"I don't know, it may be nothing, but I wonder how he knew to come see me. Have you read today's paper?"

"Yes, there was a small piece about the accident and it mentioned...wait a minute...I'll get it." Henry heard her walk away from the phone and then back while flipping through the paper "Here it is: 'A local, and much loved local, by the name of Michael Thomas Moore, was struck and killed by a car outside *The Dublin Rogue*. At this time police are ruling it an accident, but are looking for the driver. If anyone has any information....' Then it gives a number people can call if they know anything."

"I suppose Mickey could have mentioned me. Thanks Luna, you have been a big help. Could you save that for me?"

"Sure thing. Will you be around later? Mike and I thought we would come by to check on you."

"I have to head down to the library, but I should be here later in the day. Thanks again."

After he hung up the phone, he paced around a bit. It was quite likely that if Mickey did know Father Patrick, Henry could have come up in the conversation, as Mickey always told stories about his friends. Why did Henry still feel like there was something out of the ordinary? Was it something he had said?

Back and forth he paced. He imagined the greeting at the door, then the conversation. Finally Henry got it and said aloud, "I know, it always is...when one parts this earth before his time." The paper had said it was an accident. *If that was the case, shouldn't a priest conclude that it was Mickey's time?*

Henry went to his list, which only contained the one item, "Meet with Mr. Brown." He added the number two and then wrote, "Look into Father Patrick of St. Peter's Catholic Church." Henry grabbed a phone book, looked up the address, and noted it as well. Then he added his next task next to a numeral three, "Talk to Marian the librarian."

Chapter Twenty-Two

From the office window only shades of gray could be seen in the fading afternoon light. Spring was getting closer, but winter had not let go her grip on the city. A thin shapeless sky threatened to add some rain. This might wash away some of the filthy snow still lingering in the streets and on the sidewalks, but would it wash away the gray? Henry didn't think so. People were wearing their collars up to keep the uncomfortable realization that there might be one more storm left in Mother Nature's bag at bay. They walked with their heads down, their shoulders hunched, not saying a word.

Henry didn't like gray. He liked black and white; he liked blue skies and green infields; he liked order and baseball. He wanted to know the score. Who killed Mickey, and why was Katarina back? The dinner with Katarina had crept back into his mind, shoving Mickey impolitely to the side. It was wrong to let it, but reminders of her and those happy days kept nipping into his thoughts.

The worn notebook sat on his desk, with the pencil napping on top of it. They both knew it would be a while before he needed them again. There was a day, many years ago, when Henry and Katarina had been out somewhere, he couldn't remember where. They had left the bookstore or gallery and decided to walk back to Henry's place. The sudden spring storm caught them off guard.

Katarina's quick temper had her throwing a fit. She was enraged that her hairdo was ruined. She went on about it for three blocks, angry that they didn't take a cab, blaming Henry, though she had suggested the walk. She might have even cursed God, but Henry couldn't remember for sure. She finally stomped her feet while they waited at the light, and said, "Damn it, look at me! I am a mess!"

Henry smiled as he remembered his reply. It was along the lines of, "Yes, you are. I would say you closely resemble a wet rat." He had chuckled to himself, but she hadn't said anything. She was stunned. Henry had then added, "Not everyone can pull off the wet rat look, but I think it works for you." They were both soaked to the bone. It was a warm rain, unseasonably warm for spring in New York, and then there was a break in the downpour. The sunlight sneaking through the gap in the clouds made the wet street and cars seem all shiny and new. Katarina, had started giggling, slung her arm through his, and before they reached the other side of the street, the giggle had bubbled over into a full blown laughter.

Henry never told her that he had meant it, every word. He couldn't remember a time where she had looked more beautiful. There was something about having her hair soaked, her makeup running, and her rage lose control, which exposed her core, for good and bad. Henry liked truth and at that moment, she wasn't a stunningly beautiful woman because of the clothes or makeup; she was beautiful because she just was. The chaos and rain had shown him that. That may have been the moment he fell for her. Though he couldn't be sure...there were other moments too, so Henry decided to add it to the gray-area category.

Henry kept thinking about holding her hand at dinner. It was warm, soft, and familiar, though in truth, it wasn't familiar at all. It was more of a want of familiar, which was now stirring the emotions and meddling with Henry's mind. He turned away from the window, then walked to the edge of his desk, choosing to sit on the corner. To a fly on the wall, it may have appeared that he was staring off into space, but he wasn't. He was staring back in time, to their dinner, and directly into her lovely eyes. He was so focused that even his peripheral vision wasn't working.

His mind suddenly noticed something. It was a little thing, sort of fuzzy, like it was out of focus. Sitting behind Katarina, near the window at the front of the restaurant, was a man. He tried to see him more clearly, but he was just a dark mass eating a fish course. Henry wasn't entirely sure he was right about the fish course either.

Henry grabbed his sleeping notebook and pencil and ran out of the office. His coat and hat felt slighted at not being included in the outing. Once spring arrived, they would be out of action until the fall, or the odd rainy day. His progress on Mickey's killer had been minimal, at best. He was sure – or more accurately, he hoped he was sure – he would be able to piece everything together, but the whole Mickey case was out of focus too. He just couldn't wrap his head around Mickey working on something in the art world that was such a big deal, it got him killed. There must be more to it.

Henry didn't care that his light jogging up 23rd street, round the corner, and then up to the restaurant, was strange enough that people were lifting their heads out of the gray to give him dirty looks. Surely this crazy running man must be from out of town.

Henry looked around the restaurant, but didn't recognize anyone. He hadn't really paid much attention to the wait staff, but then he noticed the bartender was the same guy as before. Slightly out of breath, Henry took a moment to gather himself. With his composure returned, he asked if it was possible to find out who had been sitting at the table by the window the other night. The bartender didn't know his name, and asked one of the waiters. The waiter remembered only that he had been very generous…for a priest. Henry asked if the priest was a regular. He was not.

The pencil and notebook got it all down. There are lots of priests in New York, it could have been any of them, but his senses were telling him it was Father Patrick.

Chapter Twenty-Three

It was 6:00 when Henry decided to visit the residence of Dr. Schaeffer. He had been too busy to call Marian, though he was curious if she had found anything about the anti-thingy.

Hans answered the door. Both Henry and Hans were caught off guard. In the briefest of moments between shock and things getting out of hand, Henry decided to explain what he knew. It was possible that Henry had just stumbled upon a major piece of the puzzle, the same piece which he was expecting to meet with the next day at noon. It also crossed his mind that the expression on Hans' face, had made a slight shift from surprise to distrust, and it looked like anger was just around the corner.

"Hans, I had no I idea I would find you here. I am following up on an old case, and just today was told that Dr. Schaeffer was an expert on art. I hope you don't think…"

"Mr. Wood, I find this to be highly irregular. We have a meeting scheduled for noon tomorrow, and now I am not sure…"

A voice in the back could be heard, but was only clear to Hans; Henry couldn't make out what had been said. Hans had stopped talking, and then responded, "Yes, Doctor. Please follow me, Mr. Wood."

Henry was immediately aware he was walking through a home

unlike any he had ever seen. The décor was late 19th century wealthy-beyond-imagination, with a nod towards, early 18th century opulence.

Henry was shown to the dining room, where Dr. Schaeffer was standing by his Victrola. The man was removing the needle from Wagner's Die Feen. He carefully took off the record and returned it to its sleeve. Dr. Schaeffer then made another selection. When the music began, he spoke to Henry.

"I hope you don't mind a little music."

"I like music, though I don't know this piece."

"It is by a 19th century Russian composer and pianist by the name of Anton Rubinstein. Will you stay for dinner?"

Henry expected to ask him a few questions, but the aromas emanating from the kitchen were too enticing to resist. Hans stiffened at the request, but eased up when Dr. Schaeffer gave him a quick glance.

"Thank you, I believe I will, if it isn't too much of an inconvenience."

"Not at all Mr. Wood, though…where are my manners? I have not properly introduced myself. I gathered from the brief conversation at the door that you must be the detective Henry Wood. I am Dr. Schaeffer… welcome to my home."

Henry shook his hand, looking him straight in the eye. One can learn a lot about a person if one looks them in the eye, especially when they first meet. Henry learned nothing, and made mental a note to never play poker with Dr. Schaeffer.

The three of them took seats and a place was set for Henry. Dr. Schaeffer seemed to know the questions before they could be asked, so he did most of the talking. It was a long narrative about his home, with a little bit about Hans. He didn't really touch on why Hans had come to see him, but as dinner was finishing up, he asked Henry, "Would you like to hear a story?"

Henry had very much enjoyed dinner. Hans had warmed to him

and forgiven the intrusion. If the story was half as interesting as the dinner conversation, it would be well worth hearing. "I do like a good story. What is it about?"

"Have you heard of the 'Antikythera Mechanism'?"

The hairs on the back of Henry's neck stood up. "I was asked that yesterday. I hadn't heard of it, but I guess I have now. What is it?"

"Follow me, let's go into the library." Dr. Schaeffer gave Hans a look, and Hans made an excuse to leave. Henry followed Dr. Schaeffer to the library. As they entered, a flash of gray fur darted in front of Henry. It startled him, then a black whirling dervish shot between his legs.

"My apologies, Mr. Wood, for Jacob and Wilhelm; they are the true lords of the manor. I have had them both since they were kittens, failed to establish who was in charge, and they naturally assumed it was them. They will likely check you out, possibly give you a disapproving hiss, which shouldn't be taken personally, and then hide in the piano room. I hope you aren't allergic?"

"No, I am fine. I almost stepped on the gray one."

"Yes, he is always under foot. The gray one is Jacob."

The cats did seem to vanish, though without the hiss. Henry felt they were still watching.

Dr. Schaeffer offered Henry a cigar and brandy, which he gladly accepted. They sat down in the two chairs facing the fire. There was a brief discussion about the brandy.

Dr. Schaeffer was about to begin his story when he noticed that Jacob was on Henry's lap, and Wilhelm was perched on the top of the chair behind Henry's head, in pre-nap position. *How unusual,* he thought.

"It appears my audience is ready. They aren't bothering you, are they?"

Henry smiled. "No, I think we are ready for the story."

Captain Dimitrios Kondos made the decision in October, 1900.

They might have been able to sail through the storm, but he thought it would be safer to stay. They chose to dive for sponges. His team used standard diving dresses; the canvas suits and copper helmets allowed them to dive deeper than without the gear.

The first diver to come across the shipwreck was Elias Stadiatos. It was his description of the scene that started the questions. He said that it looked like a giant pile of rotting corpses and horses on the seabed. There was much concern on board at that, as it wasn't the first time he had been touched from the madness which comes with too much carbon dioxide. They didn't believe he had found anything… until the second diver came back with the bronze arm of a statue.

Over the next two years, a treasure trove of artifacts was recovered. There were statues, a marble bull, a bronze lyre, and even a strange box with many gears.

The work at the site was not without troubles. Several divers died from decompression sickness. This put an end to the diving.

There were many people involved in the salvage of the ship, but it was the politics of the Greek Education Ministry which caused a few of the divers to talk of mutiny. Valerios Stais, an archaeologist, was well known for having found the "Antikythera Mechanism," but what was less well known was that he felt cheated. It might have been the greatest technological discovery of the 20th century, or of any century before, and his compensation was rather paltry.

He had a brother who also excelled at diving, and was older and less honorable than Valerios. It was the brother who discovered the tube, covered in a thousand years of sea growth. It looked like a long thin rock, but he had a good eye and brought it up. He didn't tell anyone, not even his brother, at first. Several weeks of carefully removing nature's outer shell revealed a tube, carved of ebony, with a remarkably tight-fitting cap. A month later, he confided in Valerios, and they opened it together.

They were shocked. It contained a perfectly intact document.

The brothers decided not to report the find. Valerios was curious and loved documents more than the other treasures, and felt he and his brother deserved a small bit of treasure. It was the first shady thing he had ever done. Though he felt guilty about the deception, his joy at reading the ship's manifest helped him get over it.

The ship had been carrying a portion of the loot from the Roman General Sullas, in 89 B.C., and was en route to Italy. In addition to the loot, there were several items which were gifts for high-ranking officials back in Rome, including a wealthy businessman. The businessman, who was only listed by a number on the manifest, had commissioned a device for studying the heavens. The creator saw the value of it, and decided that if he were going to spend so much time inventing such a machine, it might be worth creating two. When it was completed, the first machine was such a brilliantly conceived device that those few who saw it joked that he must have gotten help from God. The second device was never shown to anyone but the man who had made arrangements to sell it to Augustus. The second machine was much more advanced, inspired by the first, and improved upon greatly.

When it came time to ship the items, great care was taken with their packing. Two men were hired to travel with them to make sure they arrived safely and to keep anyone from knowing about the second machine. Both items were listed on the manifest. There was a detailed paragraph explaining that the box destined for the benefactor was not to be touched by anyone aboard. The penalty for disturbing it was loss of one month's salary. The penalty for opening the second hand-carved ebony and ivory crate, which was for Augustus, was death. The entire crew knew better than to cross the captain or get curious about the cargo.

The container for Augustus was four times the size required to hold its precious cargo. There were three other interior boxes, lined with wool, and sealed tightly to protect it on the voyage. The precision of the machine was impressive, but the engineering and craftsmanship of the boxes was truly remarkable. The outside box was heavy and thick, with modest ornamentation, just enough to be impressive without being so awe-inspiring as to invite thieves. The interior boxes were not just containers, but locks, of a sort. Each box had a secret panel, which needed to be found in order to remove the lid. Each of the three interior boxes was made by the same craftsman, and was so precise as to be air tight.

All of these details were described in the manifest. If the ship carrying Augustus's shipment were to go down, it was believed the box would float, and thus be found and sent to Augustus. The ship did go down, but the box destined for Augustus didn't, not at first. It did float…for a while. The outer box was not quite as air tight as had been hoped. It stayed buoyant long enough to travel another three kilometers, before it sank.

The brothers, reading about the second box, knowing that it hadn't been found, devoted the next twenty years to searching for it. They found it by chance, mostly buried in the sand, a proverbial needle in a wet hay stack. They didn't know what they had; nevertheless, they bestowed the name "The Eye of God" on their find.

This is where the story begins.

Dr. Schaeffer was about to continue, when Hans entered, apologized for interrupting, and whispered something in his ear.

"I apologize, but it is a call I must take. Perhaps we can continue the story another time. It is quite fascinating, and when you know the rest of the tale, you will be better able to help me in my request. Hans will show you to the door."

The cats had both vanished when Hans had entered. Henry stood up, thanked the doctor and Hans for the dinner, and left. Henry shook Hans' hand, apologized again for the surprise, and then headed back to his office. He had a lot of writing to do.

Chapter Twenty-Four

A lovely young woman with straight dark hair and what some would describe as a European beauty sat with her friends. The bar was moderately crowded with people engrossed in their own lives. Professor Brookert sat at the bar reading while he drank a beer.

The woman was overheard saying, "I don't walk outside."

Her friends laughed. They were used to declarative statements from Celine. The aging Professor Brookert, not generally inclined to eavesdropping, had his curiosity piqued. He set his newspaper down and gave a look at the woman and her friends.

"May I inquire as to how one avoids walking outside?"

Her friends giggled. He wasn't sure if it was his age, attire, or manner of speaking which brought about their collective laughter. Their tone was light and not at all condescending, though, so he chose not to take it personally.

Celine, sensing that her friends' burst of laughter might have been misinterpreted, stood and addressed the professor. "Don't mind them. They are laughing at me." Then she told them to shush. "In the winter, it is much too icy. I choose to walk like this." Celine took a few steps on the balls of her feet.

The professor couldn't stop from smiling.

"I haven't fallen down in four winters!" she said triumphantly.

The last comment made her friends burst out in even greater laughter. People in the bar were beginning to pay attention to the commotion. It certainly seemed like there was a lot of fun happening around that table.

Celine grabbed her beer and went up to the bar. She threw herself onto the bar stool. "Does that answer your question?"

Professor Brookert picked up his own beer and clinked her glass. "Yes it does, and that was a superb demonstration, young lady, thank you very much."

"You're welcome." Celine cocked her head to one side, surveyed his horrifically unfashionable suit, and said, "You look like a professor." She smiled confidently with a nod.

Now it was time for the old man to laugh, though it was more of a chortle. "Guilty as charged, Miss."

"What do you teach?"

"I enlighten the minds of our youth regarding antiquities, old cultures, and ancient languages at NYU."

"A history teacher, eh?"

Normally having his life's devotion distilled to such a pedestrian description would have gotten his dander up, and he would have torn into the troglodyte who said it. She had not meant to offend, was hardly a cave dweller (she was too fashionably dressed), and he found her rather charming. He simply nodded in agreement.

Professor Brookert finished his beer and was about to leave, when Celine's friends insisted he join them. Two hours passed. It was a lively conversation, with Celine doing most of the talking. She had lots of stories to tell, and the professor enjoyed them all. He rarely spoke that night, but occasionally doled out a spoonful of fatherly advice when called upon.

One of the women worked at a brokerage firm, mostly getting coffee, typing up letters, and fending off advances from the bankers. "Most of the time," she giggled. The two other women were in serious relationships, lived together, and were working diligently at getting their men to propose. Both were quite sure that they would be betrothed soon.

Celine was between jobs. Two days earlier, her boss had crossed the line. She demanded respect. This part of the story she emphasized with a fist to the table. Her friends cheered. Her boss was unimpressed when she had said it to him with the same flourish, and fired her.

When Celine expressed concern about finding a job, the professor had an idea.

"I hope you won't find this too forward, but this very day…" More snickers from the peanut gallery. "…an associate of mine, a private detective, who I occasionally consult with, has expressed interest in bringing on a secretary. Though I suspect 'Chaos Manager' may be a more apt title."

Celine shot a serious look at the old man. "A detective! I would be a great secretary for a detective. Didn't I figure out that you are a professor?"

Brookert laughed, "That you did, my dear, that you did." He pulled out a piece of paper and wrote down the address and a phone number for the Henry Wood Detective Agency, and included a note to Henry. "If you give Henry this piece of paper and show up at 9:00 sharp tomorrow morning, he will grant you an interview."

Celine, showing an even higher level of enthusiasm than she had already displayed that evening, popped up from the table. "If I am going to be bright-eyed and bushy-tailed tomorrow, I best go. Night, girls. Professor Brookert." Celine flew out of the bar, and, true to form, immediately started her special winter prancing. A few careful steps later, and she was in a checkered cab.

Chapter Twenty-Five

Celine walked down the long hallway and read the words aloud on the door as she approached. "Henry Wood Detective Agency." Just hearing it seemed thrilling, certainly more so than her last job. She just hoped that this Henry Wood was more of a gentleman than Mr. Grabby Hands.

Celine was not one who was prone to stage fright. She hadn't been at all nervous when she played Little Orphan Annie as a child in the school play. Today, though, there was the slightest bit of trepidation. She really needed the job, and wanted it more than she had wanted anything in a long time. She took one last long deep breath, which calmed her fidgeting, and came to stop in front of the door. She raised her perfectly manicured hand and knocked at an appropriately moderate noise level.

She heard movement and then footsteps approaching the door. She counted the steps and quickly surmised the distance from the back office to the door. She pictured the inside and a desk, which would be hers.

"Hello, come right in. How may I help you?"

Though she didn't show it, she was a little startled by the question. The professor had told her to show up at 9:00 and to give the man the piece of paper, which she had in her coat pocket.

Celine had expected to be expected.

The smile and enthusiasm made an impression immediately, though she hadn't said a word yet. Henry took the piece of paper which had just been thrust at his chest with the speed and accuracy of an Olympic fencer. He opened it.

"I am here about the job!"

Henry held the door for her and offered to take her coat. He hung up next to his, and motioned for her to follow him into his office. They both took their seats. Henry grabbed a yellow legal pad and pencil.

"I'm Henry Wood, as you might have read on the door. What is your name, Miss?"

"Celine Spinoza."

Henry wrote her name at the top of the page. "Have you done secretarial work before?"

She spoke clearly and at a blindingly fast pace. "Yes sir. I can type 100 words per minute, take dictation, short hand, pick up dry cleaning, fix coffee, and on occasion bring in a plate of brownies which will change your perception of 'yummy.'"

Henry had delusions of note-taking, but knew that he wouldn't be able to keep up with her, so he tried to fake it.

"The brownies sound delicious."

Celine cocked her head to one side. She looked intently at Henry, and there was a long, strangely comfortable silence. "Did you really write all of that down?"

Henry looked at her, his eyes narrowed, and then he held up the yellow pad, turning it around so she could see that he had been bluffing.

"I knew it!" she said while pointing a finger. Henry thought it would have been more dramatic if she had said it in French, "J'accuse!" Still, her delivery was excellent.

"You need someone who is able to write fast enough to keep up with the speedy talkers."

Henry couldn't argue that point. He suspected that anyone trying to argue with this woman was getting in for more than they bargained for. "Tell me about yourself."

"I'm friendly, but I don't like fresh. I love baseball, but not the Yankees. I don't like cats…because of who they are. If you ask me a question, I will answer truthfully, even if I suspect you might want something else."

Having given up the pretense of note-taking, he continued, "Tell me about your parents."

"My mother is Italian, by birth and in attitude. She might be crazy. I can't imagine her having children. My father, a businessman, also loves baseball. We try to go to games often – he always buys the peanuts. I love him for that. He likes foreign women and loves Mother deeply. She loves him too, but would never admit it." Celine took a breath.

She was fearless and interesting. Henry was about to ask another question when she started up again.

"Oh, and I have a cat named Buttons."

"I thought you said you don't like cats."

"Yes. I did."

Henry expected her to elaborate, but she sat in heroic silence.

"You've got the job."

A broad smile crawled across her face. Henry began the salary negotiations phase, which frightened him a bit. She was surprisingly reasonable in her demands, and an agreement was reached. Before Henry could ask her when she would be able to start, she had popped up from her chair, gone into the outer office, and grabbed a yellow legal pad of her own. She returned to stand at the side of his desk.

"Would you like to write a letter, or have me type up the notes from our meeting? I could make coffee."

Henry's eyes darted towards the coffee maker, and she was off.

Henry brought her up to speed on the current case, explained how he had lost his mentor, and told her about the meeting with the man in the brown suit. She returned to her desk and began to furiously type notes about the case. She looked up the addresses for "Big" Mike and Professor Brookert and created files for them. There were several filing cabinets, which were mostly empty, as everything before the Tommy "The Knife" case had been destroyed in the fire. Celine asked about the lack of files, and he told her about that case. Then she typed up notes on it, too.

She is a whirling dervish, Henry thought, and then asked her to make a call to Marian at the public library, explain who she was, and ask if Marian had found out anything.

Henry was quite sure that he had just hired the hardest working secretary in the five boroughs. Soon Mike and the professor would be arriving. He stood at the window and watched the buzz of the city below. Things were starting to speed up. He just knew it.

Chapter Twenty-Six

The morning went by in a flash. Henry liked having Celine around. It allowed him to sit and think, something which he sorely needed to do. His unexpected dinner with Dr. Schaeffer was still weighing on his mind. Though, to be completely honest, it was Hans who made Henry uneasy. For an hour Henry jotted down notes about the high points he remembered from the night before. It was too bad he hadn't been able to learn more about the anti ky-thingy, or at the very least, learn how it was spelled. It would have been rude to ask, he thought to himself. No matter, soon Professor Brookert would be here, and Henry was sure that researching whatever it was would be right up his alley.

The phone rang. Henry reached for it, but Celine was quicker. She had just set a cup of coffee on his desk, and with the speed of an ancient ninja warrior, snatched the receiver from the cradle.

"Henry Wood Detective Agency: we solve your mysteries."

Henry gave her a look, and she smiled back. Celine had been there less than two hours and already she had created a tag line. Henry was getting a bargain with this one.

"May I tell Mr. Wood who is calling?" She looked at Henry, with her hand over the receiver. "It's a woman named Katarina. Would you like to speak to her?"

Henry took the phone, shaking his head a little. Celine bounded back to her desk. She seemed quite pleased with her spur of the moment, and catchy, phone-answering line.

"Hey Kat, how you doin?"

"Henry, who was that woman on the phone? She sounds young."

"She's my new secretary. I didn't ask her age."

"Is she pretty?"

Henry thought the hint of jealousy in Katarina's voice sounded strange, but it was also flattering. He knew better than to answer. Normally, he might have considered this a great moment, a sign that she felt the same way about him that he did about her, but not today. Today, there was too much going on to mess around with romance. He wasn't in the mood, and it came through in his voice.

"What can I do for you Kat? It's pretty busy around here."

"What's wrong, Henry, aren't you happy I called?" she said, feigning hurt.

"Always. I just have a lot going on. There are people arriving shortly for a meeting. I am working on...well...finding Mickey's killer."

Katarina's attempt at cute was off key, so she wished him luck on the case and hung up.

Maybe he was just getting too old for romance. Maybe the spell she had on him was weakening. Or maybe he really was just too busy. He wasn't sure and didn't care to dwell on it.

Mike arrived first and was introduced to Celine. She hung his coat up, noticed the hall tree was getting full, and said, "I'm adding 'get some additional hooks or another coat rack' to my list."

Mike and Henry were talking when Celine popped in and offered to get Mike a cup of coffee; she had just brewed a new pot. Mike accepted politely, though he was actually afraid to tell her "no". She had that effect on people. Celine said, "We need to get more coffee cups," and started writing on her pad again.

A squeal and an audible hug were heard from the outer office.

"That must be Professor Brookert. Have you met him before?" Henry said to Mike.

"Nah, we've never met."

Celine opened the door and showed Professor Brookert in. She introduced him to Mike and explained how the professor had made her new job possible. They shook hands. She got the professor a cup of coffee too, without asking. Then she left, quiet as a mouse, and closed the door behind her.

"She is something," Professor Brookert said, nodding towards the outer office. "I knew you would like her."

"Yes she is. You have a good eye. After two hours, I feel I have completely lost control of my life, and my days of sneaking in naps at the office, I fear, are gone for good."

The professor smiled, guessing Henry was right.

"I appreciate you both helping me out. The client, a Dr. Schaeffer, wants to hire me for something important. His man Hans was here two days ago, laid out some vague terms, heavy on money, light on details, and I agreed to see him today at noon."

The professor and Mike nodded, listening intently.

"Here are the highlights," Henry said, looking at his notes. "I had some luck yesterday, running down names from Mickey's notebook. I ended up at the house of Dr. Schaeffer. It was an accident, as Hans hadn't told me the name of his employer. You should have seen Hans' face when I showed up on the doorstep. Needless to say, he is a bit suspicious now. Dr. Schaeffer invited me to dinner and then started to tell me a story, which confirms my suspicions. Mickey may not have known it, but he had gotten into something big."

The professor, always one to enjoy a good tale, asked, "What was the story about?"

"He talked about something called the Anti-kythrine something or other. I still don't know what it's called. Marian, from the public library, mentioned it too, when I showed her Mickey's entry, 'Anti

Catherine. She said she would try to scrounge up some details about it."

"Do you mean the Antikythera Mechanism?"

Henry raised an eyebrow. "Yes, Professor, that's it. You've heard of the thing?"

"I have, though I can't say I know much about it. I believe that it was discovered around the turn of the century. It's almost 2,000 years old."

"Yes, well it seems that there were two of them, but I didn't get far enough into the story at the doctor's house to learn much more."

"Two of them?" the professor asked suspiciously. "I'm not sure that's true. I would have read about a second discovery."

"The doctor says the guy who found the first one found the second years later, in much better condition and didn't tell anyone. Apparently, he was upset at not having been properly rewarded from his first find."

"I suppose it is possible, but…"

"That's why I called you. I need you to find out everything you can on the first one, and any rumors you might be able to dig up about the second. And Mike, right now, I just want you to stand in the corner and look menacing. We can figure out our next move afterward."

"Sounds good, Coach," Mike said with a glint in his eye.

They heard the sounds of Celine welcoming Hans in the outer room. Lights, camera, action, Henry thought to himself.

Chapter Twenty-Seven

"Get my car!" he bellowed. Andre Garneau was in rare form and a fine Italian suit, which was wishing it was still hanging in the closet instead of being sweated through. The chauffeur bolted from the room, feeling thrilled to be out of the line of fire. He knew that once they were on the road, his dreadful boss would sit quietly, as he didn't like to talk in moving vehicles. The others weren't quite so lucky.

The verbal assault had been going on for forty-five minutes, and Garneau had worked up quite the lather. The upstairs maid, usually immune from his criticism because of the short skirt and stockings she wore, was crying. The cook's pallid face hid a deep-seeded rage – Garneau had criticized his eggs Florentine and used the word "pedestrian" in the rebuke. The butler had been severely reprimanded as well, but couldn't have cared less. The downstairs maid, well known for being weepy, was crying too, though Garneau hadn't gotten to her yet.

He was hot and exhausted. Yelling like a madman is much harder than one might think. He threw a plate, for effect, and then stormed up the stairs and slammed the door to his bedroom. There was silence from the staff. After a minute or so, they each went off to do their jobs and lick their wounds. Eventually, the chauffeur came back inside, grabbed a cup of coffee, and read the newspaper.

The letter from Father Patrick unleashed Garneau's feeling of helplessness. It was Garneau who told the priest about the rumor of someone looking into the names of the collectors, but when he read it and saw that the auction might be canceled, he was overwrought. Over the last three weeks, he had parted with three of his most prized treasures, at a minor loss. Andre had feared that the other bidders might be in a better financial position, and he didn't want to take any chances. This would be the crowning glory of his collection, and he was prepared to do anything to win. Now, he was faced with the real possibility that the item might never go up for sale at all. This was not the worst part.

Yesterday morning, knowing it was against the rules, he sent the chauffeur to see Father Patrick. He included a note begging him to go forward with the sale and offering any assistance, monetary or otherwise, to help uncover the person responsible for the mess. The father wrote back that he did not appreciate the correspondence, that there were procedures, which did not include sending notes via one's chauffeur, and if he proceeded to meddle in this matter, he would be banished from the group of collectors. Upon reading the father's reply, Garneau was stricken with disbelief. He was not used to being addressed in such a manner. He was unable to get his way and couldn't believe it. He remained in denial the rest of the day. After a bad night's sleep, he had moved on to anger.

Chapter Twenty-Eight

Hans hired the *Henry Wood Detective Agency* and handed Henry an envelope with the retainer. He then left without giving many details about the job. They waited until they heard the outside office door close.

Mike spoke up first. "Rich people are nuts."

Henry and the professor laughed. "What do you think?" Henry asked.

Professor Brookert leaned back in his chair, still trying to take it all in. "I can't believe there is another Antikythera device, and intact, too. If it's true, this may be the greatest discovery in the history of all mankind. I found it strange, however, that Hans seemed so reluctant to answer our questions."

Mike nodded. Henry stood up and walked over to get some more coffee. "It was odd. Mr. Schaeffer was very open last night." Henry shrugged. "But this is their show. If our client wants me to only speak with him, that's okay. It's his dime. The most striking thing about the job is how similar it seems to Mickey's last case."

"You think they hired Mickey?" Mike asked.

"I don't know for sure, I still haven't decoded all of his notes. Hard to say if the client name is even in his notebook. Mickey was pretty crafty. He could remember every single person who ever hired him and often didn't bother with noting the client name, at least until he wrote up the final report."

"So, what's the plan, Boss?"

"Mike, I want you to dig around and find out what you can about Hans and Dr. Schaeffer. Also, don't call me boss."

Mike winked.

The professor stood up and asked, "May I see Mickey's notes?"

Henry handed him his notebook. "I copied the three pages from his most recent case and put his notebook in a safe place."

"It looks like you decoded his list. I see that Dr. Schaeffer is on it. If he had hired Mickey, he wouldn't be on the list, would he?"

"Good observation, Professor. I still want to check out Dr. Schaeffer – Mickey may have added him to the list for the same reason."

Mike asked, "Did he check up on everyone who hired him?"

Henry laughed. "It depended. If the client was a dame, with long legs, trying to catch a cheating husband, he was off to the races. Mickey didn't care if she was on the up and up. A guy, no matter how clean-cut, was never above suspicion. He was pretty good about reading people, or at least…he used to be."

The professor got up and walked around. "It sounds like you think that whoever hired Mickey was somehow involved in his death?"

"I think that this whole thing stinks to high heaven. On one hand, it doesn't make sense that someone would hire Mickey to look into the people on the list and then kill him before he could finish. On the other hand, Mickey always said that people willing to overpay were usually up to something. On the other hand…" Henry paused and thought for a moment, "…I liked Dr. Schaeffer. My gut tells me he is on the level. Also, I think I may have had one too many hands…but I digress."

"I didn't want to say anything, but I noticed your theorizing anatomy was slightly off," the professor said with a wink.

"That's why I called you two in; I may be losing my edge."

Mike stood up. "You still have your edge, but this case strikes too close to home. We're glad to help."

Professor Brookert smiled and nodded. "Let me see if I have it straight. Right now, all we know is that there is a second Antikythera mechanism, which may be up for sale, it would likely be worth a king's ransom, and is in some sort of underground auction for the super rich. Dr. Schaeffer is one of the players, along with the other people on Mickey's list."

Henry leaned back in his chair. "Yes, but you have left out one important fact. This isn't just an antique auction for some crazy collectors. It is prized enough that someone was willing to kill, to stop Mickey from completing his job, whatever that was."

Celine stuck her head in. "I didn't mean to interrupt your meeting or eavesdrop...okay, I did mean to eavesdrop. It sounds like insider trading."

They all looked at her. She walked in and said, "The secretaries know what is going on at each brokerage firm. They always talk to one another. I see guys chatting up the girls, trying to get them to spill company beans. But we aren't as dumb as we look...well some of us are. It sounds like whoever hired your friend wanted to know what the competition was up to, to get an edge. More coffee anyone?"

There was a thoughtful silence. Celine took this to mean no, then whirled around and went back to her desk. Henry looked at the professor and said loud enough so Celine would hear, "You found a good one there. Bright kid."

"I'm not a kid...Boss."

They all laughed, then Henry got serious again. "Celine is right: it sounds like someone is trying to stack the deck in their favor. Hans and Dr. Schaeffer certainly seem to be trying to get an edge. For all we know, someone else hired Mickey to do the same. I think that both of you should check out every name on this list. Mike, you check for anything criminal; Professor, try to find out where their money comes from. Plus anything else you can learn about this mechanism would be great. And everyone, be careful…" his voice trailed off.

There was another long silence, and then Mike cleared his throat. "One more thing Henry…Luna and I have got the wake set up for tomorrow night, at *The Dublin Rogue*. You want me to start on the funeral arrangements? There are at least a half a dozen precincts taking up a collection. He had a lot of friends on the force."

Henry sighed. "It bothers me, the thought of putting him in the ground with his killer on the loose, but I guess we should. A priest came by; I think I'll go talk to him and let you know tomorrow."

The professor and Mike said goodbye, and went on their way. Henry walked out and sat in the waiting room chair. Celine was behind the desk, writing things on her notepad. "Sorry about the kid crack," Henry said.

She looked up. "Sorry about the boss crack. I heard you tell Mike. What do you want me to call you?"

"I prefer Henry, but really it doesn't matter too much. That was a nice observation you made. You've only been here three hours and I can't believe I ever got along without you. How about I buy you lunch?"

"You're not getting fresh, Henry, are you?"

"Nope, I am just getting hungry."

"Then I accept. Plus, I have a list of things we need." She ripped off the top sheet of paper, neatly folded it, and then stuck it in her purse. As they headed out, she said, "Remind me to add, 'Buy an Out to Lunch sign' for the door."

"Will do…Boss," Henry said as he locked the door behind them.

Chapter Twenty-Nine

After lunch Henry walked, alone with his thoughts, Celine having gone back to the office. His efforts to hail a cab were half-hearted at best. A few of them drove past, stopping for better dressed and more aggressive fares. He drifted along for several blocks, his mind trying to connect all of the disparate pieces. His focus reached such a state that the din of the city faded to zero. Henry didn't notice the three guys in leather coats who had been watching him since he and Celine left the deli.

In his mind, he shifted pieces, theorized, moved other pieces, and still couldn't tell what the picture was supposed to be. Eight blocks later, unable to make any progress, a thought leapt into his mind as he passed a pay phone. He picked up the receiver, threw a dime in, and started to dial the number he knew by heart: KLondike 5-5378...and then his finger hung in the air. The din of the city returned.

He hung up the phone. His brain had reflexively suggested he dial the number and ask for help, but Mickey wasn't there. He was dead. He was really dead. Seeing his body hadn't done it, spending every waking moment thinking about finding his killer hadn't made it sink in; Henry had not reached the horrible realization until the pay phone told him the truth.

The traffic, the car horns, the guy selling newspapers on the corner, all seemed loud and annoying. Henry crossed the street and caught a glimpse, in the chrome bumper of a bright green '52 Chevy, of three people behind him. He didn't turn around; he didn't need to. Henry walked for three more blocks. The windows told the tale: he was being tailed. It made him mad.

Henry was about to make a serious effort at getting a cab, when he realized he was only a block away from the gallery. Earlier he had looked through the phone book and noticed a gallery owned by some French guy who sounded like he might be related to Henri Matisse. Henry figured that he could at least fake going there, as Henry liked Matisse's work. If one wanted to learn about the art community, go to a gallery. It seemed like a reasonable move.

Henry opened the door and held it for a tiny blue-haired woman, who was leaving with a small painting carefully wrapped in brown paper. She smiled and thanked him. Her driver hopped out of the waiting black sedan, apologizing profusely for not having noticed she was coming out. There was a young couple admiring a sculpture in the corner. The rest of the gallery was empty, save for a gentleman behind a petite desk. The man, speaking with a thick French accent, was on the phone. He made brief eye contact with Henry, then returned to his conversation. Henry assumed that he had been sized up as a window shopper, which was true, so he didn't take offense.

Ten minutes passed. The couple had left, and the gentleman, who Henry assumed was Pierre Matisse, the owner, was still talking, though he was now speaking only French. A large man walked in, and Pierre hung up the phone and greeted him. "Monsieur Garneau, so good to see you again. Twice in one week, it is an honor."

They shook hands. "Yes my friend, I saw a couple of items which are not to my particular liking, but would be wonderful gifts. The people I am buying for, well, their tastes are a bit...how should I say...unrefined."

Pierre swallowed hard at the slight. "Of course, though we have many fine works, your tastes run to only the finest object d'art. I am expecting a Klimt next week though, which you might find suitable to your taste. I was just speaking with the seller when you walked in."

"Really? That would interest me. Do call me when it is available for a viewing."

Pierre nodded politely.

"I noticed the miniature Toulouse-Lautrec the other day. I think I would like it, along with the Rodin sculpture of Balzac."

Henry couldn't believe his ears. It had to be Andre Garneau, and now Henry knew what he looked like, but he wouldn't be able to get a word in with the owner, so he slipped out of the gallery and decided to head over to see Father Patrick.

Outside, across the street, the three guys stood smoking. If they hadn't been in front of a flower shop, they might have blended in, but the bright pink store front did little to help them look incognito. Henry didn't even glance in their direction; he wasn't ready to let it be known that he was onto them. He even crossed the street to be on the same side and to make it a bit easier for them.

Henry walked for about three blocks, then began to imagine a figure, maybe more, sitting in a car, smoking, waiting for his friend. Now, he was angry. He hailed a cab, hopped in, and told the cabbie to step on it. The three shadows were caught off guard. Before they could get their own cab, Henry was out of sight.

Henry tipped him an extra fiver for the quick footedness, and got out at the steps of the church. He walked inside and asked to see Father Patrick. An altar boy shuffled off to find him. Henry sat in the back. He didn't go to church often, and wasn't very religious. He considered saying a prayer, but he was still mad. Too mad to talk to God, so he just sat and watched the two people at the front lighting candles.

Chapter Thirty

The altar boy returned. "Father Patrick is with someone. He will be available in thirty minutes. Do you mind waiting?"

"I don't mind." Henry didn't mind at all. Being followed, and followed so clumsily, offended him. The calm of the church and the solace it might bring was much needed...time to cool off.

There was the faint sound of a choir practicing, though he couldn't tell from where. No doubt in a room behind a door, but the beauty of their sound reached him and it was nice. The hint of music soothed his frayed edges. There were whispers accompanying soft footsteps. The sound of muted reverence steadied his uneasiness further. Henry was glad he came in to make the arrangements.

The minutes passed by and soon Henry was being led towards the priest's modest office. Father Patrick greeted him warmly and offered a cup of tea. Henry declined and took a seat. The office was sparsely decorated, which is to say, it was almost completely barren of personal items. The Bible, sitting open on a small table, had a suspicious, though barely perceivable, layer of dust on it. Clearly this holy book was not regularly used.

The wall had but one painting. Likely painted by a young parishioner, the scene of the Virgin Mary holding the baby Jesus was competently rendered. The desk lamp seemed lonely, with nothing to illuminate. The priest removed a small black appointment book from the drawer. It had a gold cross on it.

The details for the funeral were straight forward. Henry's calm was slipping away. The suspicions about Father Patrick returned. Henry guessed it had been the priest watching him at the restaurant. The office, which the father said he had been using for years, had an unsettling feel. It was too temporary. It occurred to Henry that if he had known Latin, he might test the padre's knowledge of the Scripture, but then he would also needed to have read the Bible, so it probably wouldn't have worked. Still, the man before him did seem to know how to make arrangements for the funeral. Perhaps Henry was being paranoid.

The altar boy returned, lightly knocking on the open door. There was a gentleman waiting to give confession. Father Patrick stood, gave his condolences once more, and then shook Henry's hand.

Henry made his way up the stairs and walked towards the front of the church. The echo of a creaking noise caught Henry's attention. He turned his head to the left. It was Andrea Garneau who was seeking absolution.

Henry's little voice in his head was musing. *If I believed in coincidences, this one would be a doozie.* Henry strolled outside, and the three leather coats were just getting out of a cab. Henry played it cool. He walked, and they followed.

Two blocks, then a left, another block, and Henry stopped to buy a newspaper. He went for another fifty yards and casually turned into an alley. The moment he was around the corner, he backed up against the wall. A few seconds later the sound of hurried footsteps announced their arrival.

"Hello, boys, whatchya doing?"

The three of them stopped cold. The tall one could think on his feet, well sort of. "Nothing, daddio, just stretching out legs." He tried to sound hip and cool, but failed in both regards. It just made

Henry angrier, but he didn't show it.

"You sure seem like you were in a hurry. One could be forgiven for reaching the conclusion that you were following them. In fact, that is the very conclusion I've reached. Why are you following me?"

The tall one took out a pack of Lucky Strikes, shook it, and pulled out a cigarette. He flicked his lighter, lighting it like he had practiced in front of a mirror. He took a long deep pull and then blew it out, towards, but not directly at, Henry. His voice tried to sound tough, but was a weak attempt at best. "So, what of it?"

His buddies chuckled, which didn't endear them to Henry. They would regret laughing.

Chapter Thirty-One

"Listen kiddo, me? I don't like being followed. In fact, I really hate being followed by amateurs; it's insulting."

The three leather jackets were pretty sure they had been put down, and Henry could see them replaying it in their heads, trying to find the slight.

In a calm-before-the-storm tone, he asked, "Who do you work for?" They may not have been honor students, but his measured speech wasn't lost on them. What they didn't know was that Henry was in a foul mood and he wanted to punch a wall, but that would be unproductive.

The tall one had one hand in his pocket, the other holding a cigarette, and so was wide open. "Hey, pops, it's a free..." was all he managed before he crumpled to the ground.

Henry leaned into the punch and caught him right under the rib cage. The calm was gone and the storm was ashore.

Henry preferred clever word play to fisticuffs. He rarely carried a gun. He had been in his fair share of scuffles, though, and did some boxing in his youth, so he could take care of himself. The last time Henry was in a brawl, it was in a bar in upstate New York, but that was merely recreational.

Henry stepped on the tall one's neck. The shorter chubby thug jumped back when his friend dropped; the one whose appearance hinted at weasel, froze. Henry's left arm shot forward and grabbed the weasel's neck. The weasel grabbed the arm attached to the hand crushing his windpipe. The look in his eyes was a mixture of surprise and terror.

"I am going to beat the weasel here for a while, just for sheer joy of it." Henry smiled at the frightened weasel. The chubby one took another step back. Henry removed his foot from the gasping thug on the ground and stepped into a right jab. The force of the blow sent the weasel across the alley, bouncing off a trash can, and hitting the wall with a thud. Henry took three steps, kicked the overturned can out of the way and grabbed his neck again.

"After I get done beating the weasel into a pulp…" he paused to look at the still gasping thug on the ground.,"…I am going to have a discussion with chubby, possibly bust him up a bit…" Henry looked at the rotund thug, who had terror in his eyes.

Before Henry could finish his threat and accompanying beating, the chubby one blurted out, "Father Patrick asked us to watch you! We didn't mean nothing, mister."

Henry released the weasel, who slid to the ground, rubbing his neck. Henry reached down and pulled the tall one off the ground and patted him on the back. The chubby one picked up the weasel. "Now I am going to say this once, you understand?"

They nodded, not making eye contact.

"You are going to tell the padre I gave you the slip. You are not going to mention that I saw you following me, or say anything about this little unpleasantness in the alley. Got it?"

There was some more nodding while studying their feet. It was sort of sad, Henry thought. These three kids, probably not more than twenty-five, and this is how they handle themselves in a fight. I guess the leather jackets were just for show.

The three of them, sensing that Henry didn't have anything else to say, turned and headed down the alley. Henry picked up his hat, which had fallen off when he landed the first punch, and noticed the pack of Luckys on the ground. "Hey, you dropped something…"

They all turned around. Henry tossed the pack to the tall one. Henry looked at them, and lowered his voice. "I may have been a bit hard on you fellas. How about I buy a beer, or maybe two?"

They looked at each other; the chubby one sort of shrugged his shoulders. "I could use a beer."

The weasel cracked his neck. "Yep, I could use a cold one, too… for my eye."

Henry laughed and led the three young men out of the alley. They crossed the street and went into a seedy bar. The place was empty, and smelled of stale beer and memories erased, one shot at a time. The bartender, reading the Wall Street Journal, set it down on the bar. "How can I help you fellas?"

"Hey Mack, could I get a pitcher of Old Style and four glasses?"

The leather jackets nodded. The chubby and unscathed one smiled.

Henry grabbed the pitcher and glasses. They went to a table near the back. The tall one spun the chair around, getting some of his swagger back, and sat down.

"Let's start off with a proper introduction. My name is Henry Wood, and who are my three shadows?"

The chubby one, pouring and handing out the beers, said "Everyone except my mom calls me Pig."

"What does she call you?"

"Mostly Lawrence, unless she is sore at me…then it varies."

"Pleased to meet you, Lawrence."

The other two chuckled. "I'm Stan, just Stan," said the tall one, as he started tapping the pack of Lucky Strikes on the table.

"Stan, sorry about the cheap shot back there," Henry said with a nod.

"It's okay. You hit real good for…" Stan paused.

"...for an old man. Thanks," Henry said, finishing Stan's sentence.

The tension from the whooping was gone. "They call me Fish, though my name is Francis. I prefer Fish."

Stan lit up a smoke. Fish bummed one and lit it too. He held it between his middle two fingers, cupping his hand around his mouth as he took the drags. He thought he looked cool. Actually, he did. Stan offered one to Henry, who accepted.

"I used to smoke these. Haven't in a while."

"Why'd you quit?"

"I don't remember, just did. You smoke, Lawrence?"

"Not really. The guys give me a hard time about it."

"Why you two give Lawrence a hard time about smoking? Why does it matter?"

Stan patted Lawrence on the back. "Ah, it's nothing, we just kid around with him. If it wasn't the smoking, it'd be something else."

Henry looked at Lawrence, who sort of nodded and shrugged.

"Hey, I am sorry about how things went back there. You caught me on a bad day. Can I ask you something?"

The three of them had warmed up to Henry and were enjoying the free beer. "Sure old man, er, Henry. Sorry."

"You can call me old man, I really don't care." Henry actually liked the sound of it. "Why did Father Patrick tell you to follow me?"

They all looked at each other, then Stan said, "We didn't ask. He has us keep an eye on the neighborhood. We mostly watch for some fat guy, and let him know when he goes to the art gallery."

"You keep an eye on a guy a few night's back, about my size?" Henry didn't think these guys had killed Mickey, they didn't have it in them, but he wanted to see their reaction. They all waved their heads no.

Lawrence asked, "What do you do, mister?"

"I am a private detective."

All three of them were impressed. Lawrence said eagerly, "Is that how you learned to fight?"

"No, that was a long time ago, a different time in my life."

Now they were all in awe of Henry. They talked for another hour or so and put away a second pitcher. Henry had won them over, and they promised to not let the father know, though they didn't understand why.

Henry left the bar and hailed a cab. Across the street, smoking and reading the paper, dressed in business attire, Arthur watched Henry leave. When the cab was out of sight, he went to a pay phone and called his boss Andre Garneau.

"Boss, I did as you instructed. I tailed you all day to see if anyone suspicious was watching you. It may be nothing, but there was someone. I noticed him at the gallery and then at the church. While you were in with the padre, he left, and a few of Father Patrick's boys were following him."

"That is interesting. Find out who he is. Well done, Arthur. See you tomorrow at breakfast."

Chapter Thirty-Two

Patrick removed his collar. He was tired. The years of being someone else and playing the game were starting to wear on him. The last few days had been especially trying, and for the first time, it just wasn't much fun. He didn't like the people, he didn't like the solitude...he especially hated Garneau.

Patrick reached up under his desk, pressed the exact right spot, and a tiny panel opened up on the side. From the secret hiding spot, he removed a journal. It had the numbers of his bank accounts in Switzerland and accurate accounting of every penny he had squirreled away over the years. He flipped through the pages and read the dates. It was four years ago when he reached his own magic number, the one where he planned on retiring and giving up the life. Now he had almost doubled the number, and with this last big score, would double it again.

He turned on the radio and listened to the news. He couldn't focus; he just wanted to be done. After so many years, the thought of even one more day dealing with this last big score, was almost more than he could stand. He considered praying for strength, which made him chuckle. If the other priests only knew he was a fraud, and a damn good one, they would have a fit.

There wouldn't be time for dinner – his daydreaming about

leaving the life had run longer than he expected. Patrick needed to go out for the evening, without the risk of being stopped for a chat by a parishioner. He needed freedom to move unseen. It had been years since he had worn a disguise, but he hadn't forgotten how to do it right.

From under his bed, he pulled out his case, opened it up, and set it on the kitchen table. In a moment of inspiration, he knew the perfect disguise: he would become a rabbi for the evening. It made him laugh to think about it. It wasn't the first time he had dressed as a Jew. Back during the early days of war, he learned Yiddish, to be able to sell the part.

As he carefully added a substantial beard to his face, he remembered his days of breaking bread with the top Jewish families in Berlin. He spent a year cataloging the art and wealth in these homes. It was substantial. When the Nazis began to round up families, sending them to the camps, and ultimately to the gas chamber, Patrick changed his plan and took the opportunity to form a partnership with an enterprising sergeant and his colonel. He had originally planned on robbing the families. He figured he could get away with four to five masterpieces and they would never know. He would copy them and then switch his copies with the originals.

The Nazis deciding to round up all of the Jews presented a different set of problems. There were countless Germans who took great pleasure in burning the paintings, books, treasured photos, and clothes.

He was smart. He found two Germans, in the right position, who were far more concerned with greed than hate. Oh, they had plenty of hate, but they had much more greed. Since neither of them knew much about art, and both preferred diamonds and gold to paintings, it was easy for Patrick to divide up the treasure. The colonel was smart, very smart, and Patrick knew it. Patrick worked hard to educate his partners about the art, explaining what constituted great works and why. He then valued many of the pieces at 90% of their worth. The colonel frequently consulted others, who often knew less than Patrick, about the pieces, and the prices were usually pretty close.

What Patrick did not do was teach him about the rare exceptions, which were often the most valuable pieces. Patrick was also excelled at making a list of items to burn, which kept the troops happy and helped to avoid suspicion from superior officers. Of course, the generals received much of the obvious wealth, but Patrick was able to create a steady flow of treasure, such that everyone was happy.

He also considered his image among the most influential Jewish families. The first thing he did was to arrange for three of the most popular Rabbis to escape to France. This left fewer people to discover he was a fraud. Then he convinced the colonel to let him arrange for one of the moderately wealthy families to escape. He convinced the family to take only what they could carry. Before they left, they entrusted their most valuable possessions to their wealthy friends. Of course, Patrick knew where all of the best stuff went.

Patrick occasionally thought about all of the people who died because of him. It never bothered him once. So tonight he put the beard on again. He was meeting his contact at the docks, who would also be in disguise. The Siena was one day late, owing to bad weather. The contact was paid $20,000 as a down payment for the work he had already done. Assuming the object arrived, there would be another $200,000 to house it in a secure area. The contact, a former magician, was able to work alone, because he didn't use muscle for security; he used deception.

Patrick had used him before, and never had anyone get a sniff of where the items were located. The job required six separate viewing areas located around the city, which could house the item for a day, then it would be moved to the next spot. If needed, the site transfers could take place in hours, but Patrick preferred to take a week for the viewing. Then there would be the auction, the item in a new place, which only the winner ever knew about.

Mr. Amazing, as Patrick liked to call him, had the perfect combination of brilliance and gutlessness, which meant he would get the job done and never once consider a double cross. Patrick would be the extra labor required to move the items from one place to the next. It was his favorite part of each auction, trying to figure out where the item was hidden. He had only detected the hiding place once, and that was after Mr. Amazing had given him three clues.

So tonight they would meet, or more accurately, Patrick would head down to the docks and Mr. Amazing would find him. In most cases, despite his excellent skills at disguises, Mr. Amazing seemed to be able to find him. Tonight he hoped the rabbi garb would fool him, though he doubted it. The beard looked great. Now he only had to add about twenty years in age to complete the effect.

Chapter Thirty-Three

Henry rounded the corner. Bobby was just closing his office.

"Hey, Henry, how are you doing today? Do you need any more help?" Bobby asked.

Henry's right hand was throbbing and his mood wasn't really conducive to a long, high-speed chat with Bobby, but the hopeful look on Bobby's face made him feel a little better.

"Good to see you, Buddy. I am afraid my progress has been a little disappointing."

"You got a good one, with that new secretary. I saw Big Mike and some guy old guy in a suit leaving today. Are they helping?"

Henry wasn't in the mood to heal hurt feelings. "Yes, they are doing some legwork for me."

"I may have short legs, but I know people, who know people. I can help. I know I can. Please let me."

The rapid fire begging was more than Henry could stand and at that moment, he had an idea. Henry put on his best contemplative face, paused for effect, then patted Bobby on the shoulder. "I hadn't thought about it, but you may be able to help. Of course, you will have to keep anything you find between you and me."

"Of course!" Bobby almost shouted, then lowered his voice. "Just you and me…got it."

"I think Mickey was looking into something much more dangerous than he imagined. He had a way of smelling trouble, and would usually avoid anything too risky. But this time he got in over his head, and it cost him. I don't even know all of the players yet, but I am getting there. There is one aspect of this case, possibly the most important part, which is so shrouded in mystery…"

Henry's voice trailed off, and he looked up and down the hall, just to see if anyone was there. This was partially for effect, and it worked perfectly. Bobby was wide-eyed and listening with great intensity. "I'm having Marian at the library and Professor Brookert look into this, but I suspect you may have resources they do not." Again Henry paused. "I need you to look for anything on 'The Eye of God.' I am not confident there is much about it, but if you can find anything, it may be helpful. Right now, this thing is at the center of this mess."

Bobby seemed suddenly composed. "The Eye of God…how interesting. You are right, Mr. Wood, I do have resources."

The change from hyper to formal seemed odd, even for Bobby, but before Henry could ask him about it, Bobby was back in his office.

Henry saw there was still a light on in his own office. It was after 6:00, and he had imagined Celine would already be gone.

"Hey. I am glad you came back. I don't have a key to lock up."

"I'm sorry. I didn't even think about a key."

"It's okay. I have been busy, and I used to stay late at my old job all the time. I don't mind, but I would have gotten a little grouchy and hungry in a few hours." She smiled.

Henry walked over to Celine and removed the pencil stuck into her hair. He tilted her yellow pad, which had a massive two-column list on it, many of the items already scratched off. "Make Henry a key," he said as he added Number 37 to her list.

He tilted it back to her. While she read it, he took his own key off his ring and gave it to her.

"Thanks, but what if you need to get in before tomorrow?"

"It's okay, I'll be fine." He pulled his lock-pick set out of his pocket.

Celine displayed a hint of being impressed, but it vanished quickly. She got her coat and said, "I will be in at 9:00 sharp, if that is okay with you? We hadn't really discussed office hours."

"That would be perfect."

"There are a couple of messages for you. They are on your desk." She paused. "Mr. Wood?"

"Yes, Celine?"

"I really like my new job. Thank you."

"I really like my new secretary. Thank you."

She smiled and spun around with the grace of a ballerina. The click of the closing door, which was not too loud or soft, seemed to punctuate her first day.

The top note, which was stuck on the metal spike for holding such things, was from Professor Brookert. It just said he would call tomorrow. The second note was from Katarina. It had a number, and just said "Call ASAP."

Henry dialed the number, and the desk clerk at her hotel answered. Henry asked to speak with Katarina, and he put the call through.

"Henry?!" came the voice on the other end, sounding a little shaken.

"I got your message. I meant to call earlier, but I have been out most of the day."

"I need to see you. I need your help. Can you meet me somewhere?"

"What's wrong?" Henry said, concerned about her tone.

"I can't talk now. Meet me at *The Dublin Rogue,* in an hour."

"Just tell me what's going on?"

There was a few moments of breathing and sighs. "Henry, I need to see you in person. I'll see you in an hour."

Henry was about to ask again, but the click on the other end said "No more."

Henry paced a bit, holding the message. He had tried to find out what had brought her back into town, but each time he did, she deftly changed the subject. Henry didn't like waiting – patience wasn't one of his virtues – but he had no choice.

The other notes were from Luna and Big Mike. They would wait until morning. Henry sat down and rubbed his sore right hand. His knuckles were bruised, and it reminded him why it was better to do battle words than fists.

In the third drawer was a bottle of vodka. Henry pulled it out and poured some into his empty and, he noticed, cleaned coffee cup. As he sipped it, he noticed that Celine had added four more coffee cups to the stack. He smiled.

Why did you have to get yourself killed Mickey? he thought. Another sip, and he felt the rage boiling down in his stomach again. Henry said, as he raised his cup, "Tell you what, Mickey. I will find your killer, and you keep an eye on my friends. Whatever it was you were looking into, sure seems to have a lot of powerful people involved. You keep them safe."

It was sort of a prayer, but not really. He finished the vodka, put the bottle back, and then wiped out the cup and placed it with the others. Perhaps he would go to the bar now and a have a round or two, before Katarina arrived.

Chapter Thirty-Four

Henry walked to *The Dublin Rogue*. It was just as he remembered it. He had spent more evenings here with Mickey than he could count. Though it had been years, the faces were the same.

One by one, the familiars came over and gave their condolences. Henry appreciated each one. The peanuts on the bar were salty. Henry's tussle with the leather jackets had caused him to work up an appetite. It would have to wait.

Katarina walked in and Henry stood up to meet her. She threw her arms around him. "Oh Henry, you came...I am in so much trouble."

Henry led her to a booth in the back. Her breathing was shallow, with slight shudders, fighting back the tears. It wasn't at all like her. Henry motioned for two drinks and sat down next to her. He put his arm across Kat's shoulder.

It took her a while to get going. She stuttered, stopped and started, and then just sighed. The drinks arrived.

"Tell me what is going on."

She took a long drink and steadied herself. Henry swung around to the other side of the booth. She fiddled with her empty glass.

"The war was tragic in so many ways. The years after the war may have been worse. There are a lot of bad people in the world;

they started the war. Many of them died. Those who remained carried on. Now I am one of those people."

Henry took her hand. "I don't believe it." The words and the voice were kind. She wanted to stop there, take back what she had said, but she couldn't. It was true.

"Dear Henry, let me tell you what I have become."

Henry took her other hand and looked into her eyes…and waited.

"There are lines, black and white, which we don't cross. Wars blur those lines, greed blurs them, and in the end, my own weakness whipped them away. I don't know what is good or bad anymore. But let me start at the beginning.

"The first few years after the war, the art world was trying to regain its footing. Some painters, like Henri Matisse, had worked throughout. Others had been in hiding. The end of the war signaled the beginning of a new energy. Talented people, those who had survived, had so much pain, and they took it and put it in sculptures and paintings in ways that brought tears to my eyes.

"I learned more about art in those first few years, than I had in all my years before. I could separate wheat from the chaff better than most of the so called 'experts.' So I started to promote a few young talents, and made some nice commissions. I get to know some of the collectors. It wasn't long before I knew every major player in the art world. At least, that is what I thought. There is another world, one which is much darker, one which doesn't get written up in glossy magazines. It is the world of the private collection and their collectors.

"Because most of Europe had been looted, pillaged, and then looted again, there were lots of pieces hidden in secret places. The most talented painters, the ones who didn't catch a break, turned to forgery. They were good too, but I was better. In a three week span, I cleverly uncovered two such forgeries, and my reputation among the shadow collectors was secured. I was a straight shooter. I felt like I was doing some real good. Ninety percent of the time I could tell if it was real or forged, and my explanation would steer the buyer down the right path. On a few occasions, when I didn't know, I told them so. Then I told them who to contact, to find out for sure. Even this furthered my reputation.

"Then a man came to me, he was hunting for a particular piece, which was rumored to be hidden in Romania. He asked that I go check it out. The piece was famous and had gone missing during the war. Before we went to Romania, we went to Vienna. He took me to dinner, introduced me to some wealthy people, and then I got to see a 'private collection.' As we were walking down the long hallway to the secret room, which housed the treasures, he reminded me that I was not here to validate any pieces. I should just smile and gush.

"It was an impressive collection, to say the least. I won't bore you with the details, but there were three pieces which I knew had been stolen during the war. One of them was the very piece we were on our way to see in Romania. Our host knew of my vocation, and stood next to his prize. He asked if I would mind, as a courtesy, to give it a quick look. The brushwork was perfect, the frame was of the right age, even the canvas was beyond reproach. When the host looked away, I took a tiny straight pin, and poked it through the corner of the canvas. The oils were not yet dry. This was not a 300 year old painting, probably closer to three months. He asked me for my opinion, and I said honestly, I had never seen anything like it.

"I didn't lie; it was the finest forgery I had yet seen. My benefactor seemed concerned, until I explained my findings to him."

Henry ordered another round when the bartender stopped by the table.

A beat cop came in and talked to a few of the other cops in a hushed tone. Most of the bar was getting up and putting on coats, girlfriends and wives were being kissed goodbye, and out they filed.

Henry grabbed the arm of a young one who had just gotten his coat from the back, and asked, "Hey, what's going on?"

"Some rich guy, a friend of the mayor, just got his head bashed in. It's all hands on deck."

The Dublin Rogue was eerily quiet after everyone had left. Henry got up and put four bits in the juke box and returned to the table with two more beers. Katarina took a drink, lit a cigarette, and took a long, slow drag. Henry accepted when she offered one. He slid it behind his ear. "For later, thanks. Now, you were telling me tales of your dark and mysterious life."

A sad half-smile crossed her lips. One more pull and a look off into the distance. *Was she looking back at the good days, or forward to what might come?* Henry didn't know. "Where was I?"

"You had just explained to your benefactor that the painting was a fake."

Katarina looked across the table, into Henry's caring eyes, and began again. "Yes, so we went to Romania. In a real life dungeon, deep under a castle, there was a room with the painting. It was the real McCoy. After the viewing, we had a wonderful dinner with our charming host, and then we left. I remember the rush. It was exhilarating beyond anything I had ever known. Better than even…" She raised one eyebrow.

Henry knew she was going for levity, perhaps she needed to, because he could see where the story was going. A brief smile, with no return eyebrow play, and a drink of beer would be all she would get. "Tell me about this benefactor of yours."

She turned her head towards the bar and crossed her long legs, as she brought the cigarette to her mouth. Another long pull, her eyes looking at nothing in particular, she answered, "His family name was Pergerinus, and he had grown up a gypsy, wandered about most of his life, and eventually changed his name to marry money. He changed it back when most of her family was killed during Dresden bombings, leaving him but one obstacle between him and obscene wealth. His wife died of grief. Or that is how he told it. I didn't ask for details."

She tapped out her cigarette, took a drink, and looked back at Henry. "He had connections all throughout Britain, Europe, Russia, and North Africa. At first I looked at the evaluations as simply jobs. They weren't any different than if I had done them for a legitimate art house. But they were different. Their pay was much higher, and eventually he started to play both sides. Sometimes I convinced people they had fakes, in order for…"

She paused.

"It is hard, Henry, to tell you about this."

"It's important I know what is going on, if I am going to help you. Please…"

"Mr. Pergerinus would send in a shill to buy the real art, which I deemed fake, at a modest price. The rube would think they had gotten a deal, considering it was a worthless fake."

Henry looked up for a moment. In a whisper, "Do you know the guy at the bar?"

The bar was mostly empty, and Katarina couldn't see him from her side of the booth. She grabbed her purse and went to the ladies' room. As soon as she did, the man folded up his paper, put a fin on the bar, and headed out into the night. Henry waved the bartender over.

"You know that guy who just left?"

"Nah, never seen him before. He just ordered one beer, read his paper, a racing form I think, then left. Probably waiting for his girlfriend to sneak away from her husband or something." He chuckled. "We get quite a few people in here who are just killing time. Can I get you anything else?"

"No, we probably need to get going. I'll see you tomorrow…we will toast to Mickey until we can't see straight."

"You bet we will." He wiped off the table and took the empty glasses back to the bar.

Katarina returned with a concerned look on her face. "I have seen him before. I think he may be one of the guys following me."

"Grab your coat. You are staying with me tonight."

Normally she would have made a remark, but she did as she was told. Katarina looped her arm through Henry's as they walked out of the bar.

"I have a place we can go," he said. "It is safe; very few people know about it."

They didn't talk much during the walk to the car, or the drive to Brooklyn. Henry drove in circles some, looking for tails, and eventually wound his way to his house. It had been a few days since he had been back home. It was unusual for him to stay in the city more than one night in a row. All his tools and woodworking stuff were in Brooklyn, and most nights that was how he chose to unwind.

* * *

From a phone booth down the street, Arthur put down his racing form and called in to Mr. Garneau. "I did as you said and continued my observations, but there is an interesting twist. I will tell you in the morning, at breakfast."

Arthur lit up a cigarette and then walked a few blocks before hailing a cab. He had the cabbie drop him off outside of the Ritz, then a few minutes later, hailed another cab. Arthur was a cautious man; much like Henry, he didn't like being followed. One never knew who was watching in the night.

Chapter Thirty-Five

One sixtieth of a second passes, and the smallest fraction of a moment is imprinted on a negative; one can print up a photo to help them remember. Life is made up of these moments, most of which fade over time. It helps to have an album.

Henry didn't need a camera. They had driven to Brooklyn, and Katarina had gotten to the part of the story where she thought she was in danger and being followed. Of course, the reason they were in Brooklyn to begin with, was that Henry had already figured it out.

Katarina came out of Henry's bedroom, having borrowed one of his shirts. Her hair was down, and there was a relaxed look on her face as she padded into the kitchen in her bare feet. Katarina started to make an omelet.

Henry sat at the table and watched. She had great legs for omelet-making. Katarina was tired of talking, so she hummed instead. The light sizzling sound of bacon seemed to fit with her rendition of "Mr. Sandman." It was a huge omelet. Henry ate. She watched him and nibbled occasionally.

They kissed.

Many years later, it would be the late night omelet he shared with her, not the bed, which he would remember most fondly. Her nibbling, while all around hung a comfortable silence, combined to form a moment for which all others would be judged.

She was still sleeping when he got up. Henry wandered down to his shop. The tools were there waiting for him to return, as he had left so abruptly the other evening. Henry held a chisel and tapped it lightly against the bench. He stood and looked at the closet.

The closet, which he had never fully understood, and, strangely, never questioned, had been quiet for a couple of months. Henry had meant to ask Sylvia's father if he was behind it. He had been doing experiments, and it was the only remote explanation. How could there be a closet in which things seem to appear from nowhere? Not just nowhere, but from the future. It seemed that every time he needed a little bit of help to find the next clue, there would be "presents" from the future. It was so strange, so beyond belief; he figured there was no point wasting time trying to uncover the mystery. Plus, he liked the stuff it gave him. He couldn't have solved the last case without the closet's help.

Henry opened the door. On the floor were a couple of newspapers. Not at all typical for the closet, but Henry bent over and picked them up. The date was March 21, 1955. Henry flipped the top paper over and looked at the second one; it was from the day before. This was almost stranger than getting stuff from the end of the century. Why would there be current papers in the closet?

Henry was in too good a mood to question anything too deeply. So he set the chisel down, flipped off the light, and headed back upstairs. It was just 7:00 a.m., but there was a lot to do, before the wake. Henry felt as though he would conquer the world today… but not before a couple of bagels. He wrote a note telling Katarina he was heading out to forage for the morning meal, and left it on the table next to the two papers.

Henry had to shield his eyes when he stepped out onto his front porch. The morning sunlight caught him right between the eyes. It had been dreary for about 600 years, and suddenly it was warmish, probably 50 degrees, and there might have even been a bird or two crooning. Henry drove around for a short while, taking in Brooklyn and all of its greatness. He had several favorite bagel haunts, including one run by a Polish couple, who always made him laugh.

The Krakow Bakery would do nicely, he thought, and turned on the radio as he headed off in search of baked round goodness. Actually, that was the wife's motto, though Henry was never sure if she was talking about the bagels or herself. He picked up two dozen, several types of cream cheese, and some lox. Henry decided he would take the rest in to the office for Celine to enjoy and offer with her coffee. This made him think of coffee. So he went to the grocery store and picked up several choices, some filters, and some tea. He was quite sure his new secretary/boss would approve.

The hint of spring in the air told Henry that today would be the day he made a breakthrough in his case, or cases. Did he have one or was it two, or perhaps three, if he counted the guy tailing Kat? Hell, he would solve them all, as a group or individually; it didn't matter.

Henry returned to his humble abode and found Kat sitting at the table, reading the paper.

"You are my hero. You save me from the bad guys and then feed me. Will you be slaying a dragon in my honor?"

"Perhaps after breakfast, though I do need to get into the office. Could I deal with the dragon later?"

She shrugged her shoulders. "Sure, whenever you like."

Henry set the bagels down and started to brew some coffee.

"This must be where they were going to last night," she said.

"Oh, what is that?"

"It says here, a Mr. Brown, of Park Avenue, was beaten to death in his home. They think it happened yesterday afternoon, though time of death hadn't been determined officially." She paused, "I wonder what he did? It doesn't say, but the name sounds…"

Henry had stopped cold. "May I see that please?"

Katarina had a distant look on her face, like she was trying to remember something, and handed him the paper.

Henry sat down and read the article. It was the same Mr. Brown from Mickey's list. Henry's stomach did a flip. He opened the other paper, and then found the article about Mickey. When had these arrived?

He could barely breathe. Had they been sent as warnings? Was he supposed to have saved his friend and the nice man in the brown suit? Suddenly, Henry's world was in a fog. He kissed Katarina on top of the head and told her that he was going to take a shower. He needed to get back to the office, for only work would keep him from going crazy, and he knew it. This moment he wouldn't forget, either.

Chapter Thirty-Six

Henry was not surprised to see the office lights were on. He was right on time, but had had a sneaking suspicion Celine might beat him in today. She did seem eager. He opened the door, and she greeted him with a smile.

"Good morning, Celine," he said, adorning a much cheerier disposition than he felt. The discovery of the newspapers had kicked a hole in his psyche.

"Good morning, Mr. Wood. There is already a message for you. It is from Mike and seems urgent; it came in about ten minutes before nine."

"What time did you get here?"

"I was just walking in the door when it rang."

Henry set the bagels and other things he had purchased on the corner of her desk. He flung his coat and hat on the chair in his office and sat down to return Mike's call. Celine gave him a dirty look as she picked up his coat and hat.

"Hey, Mike, I just got in."

"This mess is heating up, Henry. Did you see the news about Mr. Brown?"

"I saw the morning paper. They didn't print much in the way of details though."

"Yeah, it was made to look like a robbery, but I'm not buying it."

"Did you go to the scene?"

"I got a heads-up from one of the guys downtown. I went into the station after our meeting, just to ask a couple of the old timers if they knew anything about the guys on our list. I didn't get much. When the call came in, my buddy gave me a ring."

"So tell me what happened."

"There wasn't any sign of forced entry, so he must have let him in."

"Him? You know it was a guy?"

"Well, I guess I can't say for sure, but there were footprints in the blood. It looked like a man's shoe. I guess it could have been a woman wearing it. I shouldn't assume."

"Don't worry about it…first day on the job."

Mike gave a snort. "It appears he was hit with a pipe or a bat, though I suspect the pipe is more likely, as Mr. Brown might not have opened the door to someone with a baseball bat. Again, it is an assumption, but I suspect it was something smaller he, or she, might carry under their coat."

"That is good reasoning, Mike. I agree."

"The thing is, Henry, we have another issue. The captain got word I was poking around. He knows why I took my vacation. He didn't mind before, but now I show up with a list of names, and a few hours later, one of them is dead. He wants to see you down at the precinct…immediately. Correction, he wants to see us immediately."

Henry thought for a moment and decided it would be best to get it out of the way. "I'll be right down."

Celine was enjoying a bagel when Henry finished with the call.

"I have to go down to talk with Mike's boss. I don't know when I will be back. It may be a while." Henry took two cards out of his wallet. "I may call later; if I do, this is a bail bondsman, and the other is my attorney."

Celine did not like the sound of that. "What happened?" she said, sounding shocked.

"One of the guys we've been looking into got his head bashed in. I'm not sure when it happened. Depending on the time, I may or may not have an alibi, and if I don't, I may need to have you make some calls."

"I will bust you out of the hoosegow myself."

Henry smiled. "Just make the calls." He was just about out the door. "Oh, I have one more guy who is going to do some poking around. His name is Bobby; he is just down the hall."

"I've met Bobby. He is adorable...and chatty."

"Good. I'll tell him that he may use my office to make calls, if he wants to. I suspect many of his contacts are long distance."

"I understand, Boss."

Henry stopped in to see Bobby, told him the score, and asked if he wouldn't mind hanging out in his office. Bobby was thrilled. He grabbed an armful of old books and scampered down the hall. Henry went to find a cab.

Chapter Thirty-Seven

Henry wasn't anxious to meet the captain. He knew how it would go: there would be some yelling, a bit of intimidation, and a feeble attempt to get Henry to share what he knew. The captain would expect Henry to deny knowing anything. Mickey always said, "Don't let the good guys get in the way of stopping the bad guys." It had never made any sense to Henry, as their cases rarely were about "stopping the bad guys," unless one counted a guy stepping out on his wife. Henry prepared for the worst.

Mike arrived just as Henry's cab was letting him off at the curb.

"Hey, Mike. Sorry if I've gotten you in hot water."

"Nah, don't worry about it. Everyone wants to get the scumbag that ran down Mickey, even the captain."

Henry and Mike walked through the precinct. They shook some hands and talked with a few of the guys. The general feeling among the men in blue was positive. Henry was doing God's work.

They closed the door, and the captain motioned for them to take a seat. He started to talk, but stopped, pacing behind his desk. Then he took a full yelling breath and clinched his jaw…but no yelling came forth. He sat down and leaned forward on his desk. Henry and Mike didn't say a thing.

"When I was a rookie, I wasn't doing so well. I walked in on a guy holding up a liquor store and froze, and he ran out the back. I chased him, but slipped on some garbage in the alley, and knocked myself out. Two weeks later, the same guy…he got away again. I was the laughing stock of the precinct. My old man was a cop, died on the job in July 1919. I couldn't get the thought that he was up in heaven, shaking his head in disgust, out of my mind. Even back in the day, *The Dublin Rogue* was a cop bar, and that's where I met Mickey. I was wallowing in self pity, drinking myself blind. He listened."

Henry shot Mike a quick look. This wasn't going as he expected.

The captain stood up again and looked out of the window. "Mickey went out the next day, figured out who the guy was, basically solved the case, and then gave me a call. I got the collar and restored my honor. Mickey never told anyone it was him. He never even mentioned it to me afterward. When I tried to thank him, he waved me off."

Henry said, "He always looked out for me; I am not surprised he helped out. He just did stuff like that. It's who he was."

The captain turned back from the window. "I want to be out there with you two, hunting the bastard down, but I can't. I got to do it by the book. I got the entire precinct looking for this bum, as if he ran over one of our own…which…I guess he did. The problem is we got nothing but a few paint scratches. Then my man here, who you commandeered, shows up with a list of names, and a few hours later, one of them is dead."

Henry saw what was coming, the accusation, and he was ready. "Captain, I didn't—"

"Don't be stupid, or think I am. Mickey taught you better than that. I know you didn't do it. What I don't know is how Mr. Brown and Mickey are connected. I don't want to hear any of your bullshit about 'not knowing anything' or—"

"Captain," Henry opened his notebook, "let me bring you up to speed." He tore out the two pages which he hadn't decoded. Sliding them across the desk, he said, "I copied these from Mickey's notebook, which I lifted off the body." Henry paused for yelling.

The captain said, "Go on."

"Mickey loved secret codes and took lots of notes. The problem is he had a fantastic memory and rarely needed to look at the notes again. This meant, he could write in code, and it could be extremely strange and bizarre, because he didn't fear forgetting how to crack it again. I haven't determined who his client was, not even close. I broke the code for the list of names, but still don't have a clue about these other two pages."

"If we knew who the client was, we could find out what was going on,." Mike added, and the captain nodded in agreement.

"I don't know if the client name is on the list, though I don't think it was Mr. Brown, as I spoke with him."

"You did? When?"

"Two days ago, at his office. Mickey had been trying to get in touch with Mr. Brown. He didn't know why. I was able to figure one thing out: this whole thing revolves around some big underground art auction." Henry left out the details about the Eye of God, as he wasn't ready to lay all his cards on the table, but he showed most of them.

The captain sent the two pages to be looked at by a couple of detectives. Henry didn't mind; he had the originals. The phone rang, and the captain told them to hold his calls. Henry laid out everything he had done since they told him Mickey was dead. Well, everything but his time with Katarina. The captain never said a word when Henry mentioned breaking into Mickey's place. He never yelled or threatened. He just listened. When Henry was done, the captain gave him a long look.

"You remind me of Mickey. He finds a thread, pulls it, and sees what unravels. I'll have somebody look into these three lads in leather. You may not have all the answers, but it seems you have been asking some of the right questions." He started pacing again.

"If Mickey died because of some snooty art sale…"

Henry and Mike sensed the meeting was over. The captain was going to have his men focus on the Brown murder and run down all his known acquaintances. They would try to dig up something on this underground art ring. Henry and Mike shook the captain's hand and agreed to share any new leads.

Henry and Mike shared a cab back to the office. "That didn't go how I expected," Mike said as the cab pulled away.

"I know. It was strange. You said he was fuming."

"He was, but then he starts into his story, and I guess something changed for the captain."

Henry and Mike sat in silence for the rest of the ride. They hadn't noticed the cab behind them or the man who was now tasked with recording Henry's every move. He was remarkably adept at being a shadow.

Chapter Thirty-Eight

The door was answered by a woman with a thick accent. She didn't say much beyond hello. Dr. Schaeffer was waiting in his library and greeted Henry warmly.

"I am pleased that you accepted our offer. I am sure your help will be invaluable. May I offer you a drink?"

"No thanks, Doctor, but a glass of water would be nice."

Dr. Schaeffer poured a glass from the pitcher at the bar while motioning for Henry to take a seat. "Before I continue with the story of the Eye of God, or more aptly, the legend of it, let me outline the details of the job."

Henry took out his notebook and settled into the high back leather chair.

"As you know, I am an art enthusiast. There are many of us, and we enjoy the competition of the auction. An afternoon of bidding at Christies or Sotheby's is an extraordinarily pleasant diversion. Obtaining an object of beauty is one of my great pleasures in life. But that is only half of the story." Dr. Schaeffer took a sip of his drink. "The other half requires some explanation."

There was a light knock at the door, and Hans leaned in. "Dr. Schaeffer, if you don't need anything else this afternoon…"

"That is fine, Hans. Henry and I have much to discuss. I will speak with you tomorrow."

* * *

Hans gave Henry a polite, albeit cold, nod and then closed the door. A moment later, the front door could be heard opening and shutting.

Hans walked across the street and down the block. He entered a bakery, where a man waited for him. "They will be there for hours. I propose we head up the street."

"I could use a pint."

Hans and Arthur, unbeknownst to their employers, were old friends. They also had their own agenda. They sat in the corner, away from prying ears, and spoke in hushed tones.

Arthur started. "Patrick would have a fit if he knew what was going on."

Hans laughed. "The father is a prick, wearing his collar and acting pious all the time. But we know his skeletons, don't we, my friend?"

Arthur and Hans clinked glasses. Arthur asked, "So, what do you know about this Henry guy?"

"He is not to be underestimated. He was Michael Thomas Moore's apprentice and seems much cleverer; plus he has help, something Mr. Moore could have used."

"So where are we?"

"The Falcon assures me that everything is on schedule, despite the Eye still being at sea. We are a few days from never having to work again. I must admit, I will miss Dr. Schaeffer, but it will pass. How is the whale?"

"He is as disgusting as ever." Arthur shook his head. "He is almost manic over the thought that the good father may call off the auction. His paranoia is beyond the pale, although, I guess it is reasonable in this case."

They laughed again.

* * *

Dr. Schaeffer was just finishing up with his childhood and Henry was getting a little impatient, but then the story got interesting. "So there I was with a nice practice, and Hitler starts World War II. Before I knew what had happened, I was practicing my trade in the Luftwaffe." He stood up and went to the bar, refreshed his drink, and continued. "There were many evil people, on both sides. I had devoted my life to the healing of the sick, and suddenly death and cruelty were everywhere. I suppose I shouldn't complain; my parents were safe, for a while at least. I am ashamed of what Hitler did in the name of the 'Master Race.' When I learned of the camps, I started to think of redemption."

"Redemption?"

"Yes. One man can only do a little, but I was determined to devote my life, and considerable resources, to do as much as I could. I had only a few friends during the war, but they were well connected. We would gather, and they would tell stories of the plunder and looting of the Jews. The world's finest pieces of art were being stolen, hidden, and sometimes burned. The pieces which did survive, hidden away in secret spots all across Europe, are still mostly there. I decided to devote my life to returning these paintings, sculptures, and other treasures to their families. Sadly, many of them are still lost, but I have managed to acquire and return seventeen pieces."

"You are buying art and giving it back?"

"Yes. There are a number of Jewish organizations who are searching for the stolen treasures. They have been compiling lists of missing pieces since the war ended. I have made a friend with a rabbi, who researches each piece I buy. On those occasions when he has determined that the piece was stolen, he returns it anonymously to the rightful family."

"I am impressed," Henry said, and he was.

"Don't be. I am only doing what must be done. The problem is that there are many people who don't care if there is blood on the work they buy. Art collectors are soulless. This brings me to the Eye of God, a truly unique opportunity."

"Was it stolen?"

"Well, not in the same way as the other pieces. But it has caused quite a stir, and I intend to use this to my advantage."

The woman with the accent brought in a tray of food. She asked the doctor if there would be any guests for dinner. Henry declined when invited, explaining that he had a previous engagement.

Henry enjoyed a few of the tiny sandwiches the woman had brought in. Dr. Schaeffer seemed ill at ease. "I don't believe in fairy tales Mr. Wood. My own fascination with this..."

Henry looked up, sensing the change in moods. "...Eye of God?"

"Yes, I hate even using the name. Do you recall the story of how the brothers found it? I believe that's where I left off."

"Yes, I remember," Henry said as he was suddenly aware that the cats were once again seeking his attention. "They are Jacob and Wilhelm?"

Dr. Schaeffer smiled. "Yes, the nosy one, trying to wiggle his way onto your lap, is Jacob."

Once Jacob was done settling into Henry's lap, and the purr had died down to a murmur, Dr. Schaeffer continued. "For several years after the find, the two brothers hid it in their uncle's house. The uncle had a fascination with clocks, and liked to take them apart and study the gears. It required a year to uncover the secret to opening the inner two cases. When they pulled the device out of the box, it was a mechanical marvel. It is here that my story becomes, well...unconfirmed."

"This is interesting, sure, but I fail to see what you hired me to do."

"Please, if you will indulge me a little further."

"Yes, of course. Please continue." Henry rubbed Jacob's ears. It was well received.

"There is so little known about the item since then. It is believed a covenant was created. Nobody knows how many people were involved. It certainly must have been a fair number, probably relatives and close friends, because the item is rumored to have changed locations on a weekly basis, never returning to the same hiding spot. Over the years, Valerios devoted his life to understanding the purpose of the mechanism. I don't know if he ever uncovered its true purpose, but I do know some of the ridiculous claims which have been made. Though there are few people who are aware of the Eye of God. Those who are have speculated that it is a device for calculating the precise moment when the stars and planets are arranged in a fashion, which will allow for communicating directly with…"

Henry didn't say a word.

"…with God." Dr. Schaeffer rubbed his face. "I don't know, it all sounds so crazy, especially when I say it aloud. But there have been some strange cases where those who have tried to use it have had life-altering experiences. Supposedly the first time Valerios used the machine, there were five people present, and at the hour predicted, he spoke into the small opening which appeared. Two doors opened up, and Valerios requested an end to the drought, which plagued the farmers. Those present were all in agreement that it was a selfless request. That night, after two consecutive months without rainfall, they received almost twelve inches. The resulting flash floods destroyed many of the farms, left hundreds of people homeless, and took the lives of six people."

"Be careful what you wish for…" Henry said with a sigh, not sure if he should believe the story.

"Indeed. This one act, or more likely, coincidence, put the fear of God into the group protecting the mechanism. They quickly evolved into a society of men devoted to the protection of this powerful artifact. Though locals knew of the society, they didn't know the name, and we still don't today. Or at least, I haven't been able to learn the name. It doesn't matter. There is another story, when one of the society members, in great debt, about to lose his family pottery business, asked for help. The next day he received an order which would bring him vast riches. A week later, his wife died in a freak accident with one of the kilns. From that point forward, the locals would attribute every serious catastrophe and triumph to the secret order. Most of the other stories seem only loosely connected to the machine or its protectors, so I won't go into them. I honestly couldn't say if any of the stories are true, partially true, or just the product of simple minds, but I do know that the perceived powers make it extremely valuable. It will also make The Eye more dangerous than you imagine."

"Dangerous, how?"

"It's the sort of relic that entire religions are based upon. It's the type of thing which could raise an army or destroy one. And that's if none of the stories are true. If it's as they say, well then, my mind can't begin to comprehend the power. I've hired you to uncover the truth about the item and to find out who is after it."

Henry set Jacob on the floor and stood up. "Why did you hire me, specifically?" It was time to find out if Dr. Schaeffer had hired Mickey.

"I hope you won't take offense, but you were not my first choice. I hired another private detective, and he had been working on the case when he was killed. I believe he was hit by a drunk driver or something. The papers didn't say."

"Did you know that I used to work for Michael Thomas Moore?"

The look of surprise was genuine. "I did not. Admittedly, I've been relying on Hans. I sent him out to find a new detective after he informed me of the accident involving Mr. Moore."

It seemed to be the truth. Henry had his first answer. It provided little consolation. "What were the instructions you gave Mickey?"

"Mickey...ah yes, Mr. Moore. I told him the story and then

asked the same of him, the only difference being the time. We are but a few days from the sale now, so it's much more urgent that you get me answers. There is one other thing; I would like you, and your professor, to accompany me to the viewing. Hans tells me that he's an expert in antiquities."

"I am not sure this thing falls within his area of expertise, but he'll be thrilled to see it."

"If nothing else, he can verify the ages of the containers. This would be invaluable to me. To be honest, I would be relieved to find that this whole thing is a hoax."

Henry shook his hand and gave both cats a goodbye pat. Henry liked Dr. Schaeffer, almost as much as the cats liked Henry.

Chapter Thirty-Nine

If he answered on the third ring, it meant trouble; if he let it ring past three and then answered, then all was on schedule. If he didn't answer, Patrick would try again, just to be sure. This was a system devised long ago – as with everything, he liked to be careful. In general, they wouldn't talk during the calls, unless there was something important. Tonight, Patrick had to alter the plans. On the fourth ring, Randy, the 'Remarkable,' answered.

"I have an update."

"Oh?"

"We will only need five viewing areas. One of the interested parties is no longer collecting." *Or breathing*, he thought.

"You're not trying to cut my fee?" Randy asked.

"Your fee will remain the same. Are you ready for the arrival?"

"I have the first four locations complete and the last two – well, one, I guess now, will be done tomorrow. It's really too bad: the sixth spot was quite clever. My personal favorite."

Patrick smiled. "My friend, you are a true artisan." An idea suddenly flashed across his mind. "If you want, you could finish it, and we could meet there for the final payment. I would love to see it."

This appealed to Randy; he was a complete narcissist and loved to show off. "I'll finish it. You are paying for six, so it only seems right. It's almost show time, so I am off. Check in after 10:00."

Patrick was satisfied.

Randy hung up the phone and stood looking out of the 4th floor warehouse window.

In his right hand, he cut a deck of cards over and over. The bottom two floors were rented by a company who sold cheap tourist gifts. Most of the stuff was crap, so there wasn't much security, and it was likely insured for more than it was worth. The third, fourth, and fifth floors had been vacant for months. The fourth floor, divided into two rooms, was perfect for receiving the shipment. Randy had set up a card table in the room to the right of the freight elevator. On the table sat two envelopes and a bottle of ouzo. Patrick had sent the bottle of liquor with the money, figuring their Greek friends probably needed a shot.

Randy liked the idea of the booze, as it would distract them. Each envelope had $15,000, twice the agreed upon payment. Patrick had figured the poor schmucks might want more after their horrific sea adventure. He decided they had earned the bonus. Randy agreed, but considered taking half, knowing that they wouldn't be expecting the bonus. Then he thought better of it. Father Patrick had a way of smelling deception. It wasn't worth the risk.

The truck pulled up without its lights on. *Good, they can follow directions,* Randy thought. He watched them get out at the loading dock.

* * *

Speaking in Greek, the tall one said, "I need a drink."

"This wasn't worth it. We should ask for more money. We could have died," the younger one complained.

"Yes, maybe, but what are we going to do if they say no? Take it back? Not on your life."

"You are right, my friend, this box is cursed. We should be

paying them to take it."

They both laughed, though not too heartily, as sea sickness had taken its toll. The crate was hoisted onto the cart and wheeled to the freight elevator. The siren from a distant ambulance barely disturbed the eerie quiet.

* * *

The aged elevator cables creaked as it lifted the two men and their precious cargo.Randy new they were on their way. Both men look surprised to be greeted by only one man. They expected a small army.

"Hello, my name is Randy. Do you speak English?"

The tall one looked at his friend, who said, "I do. He doesn't. He is old."

Randy shook both their hands. "You had a rough trip, boys, but it's almost over." His easy tone seemed out of place.

"Where do we put it?"

Randy led them to the room on the right. The vast open spaces seemed odd for only one box, but they did as they were told. It took both of them to lift it. They placed the crate by the center pillar on the far side of the room. The silence, except for the squeaking cart wheels and the two men's footsteps across the wooden floor, was unsettling.

Randy seemed to walk like a ghost. "Please take the cart with you. I have your money in here." The two men followed, leaving the cart in the hall. Randy pointed to the table. A desk lamp shone on the two envelopes next to the bottle. The tall one said something to his comrade, in Greek. Randy guessed it was regarding the bottle, as they both seemed happy, and the smaller one patted his friend on the back. "Please, count the money. As you will notice, there is a bonus. You have suffered much on your trip, and earned it."

* * *

The one who could speak English translated what Randy had

said to his friend. Both men opened the envelopes and thumbed through the bills. The tall one turned around, grabbing the bottle. They were alone. He opened the bottle and took a pull, then handed it to his friend. They both walked towards the door, the bottle passing between them. "Hey, tell your boss that we appreciate the…" The shorter one poked his head into the other room, expecting to see the man inspecting the massive box, but he wasn't there. The room was empty, no sign of the man or the box. He tapped the taller one on the shoulder to show him. They shrugged their shoulders, grabbed the cart, and got on the elevator. The Greeks were glad to be done bearing gifts and couldn't care less where it had gone.

Chapter Forty

It's hard to say how many people showed up to *The Dublin Rogue*, but they all had the same solemn look on their faces. A look Mickey would not have tolerated. At the end of the bar, a large photo of Michael Thomas Moore greeted the guests. It was the same with each person, the moment they saw Mickey's goofy expression – a smile and a heavy sigh.

Tommy Dorsey's version of "I'll Be Seeing You" brought a roar from the crowd. It was one of Mickey's favorite songs and his favorite argument. Half the regulars preferred "The Ink Spots" with Bing Crosby's version, and Mickey would routinely rally the other half in a rousing debate. Tonight, the Bing Crosby supporters, led by officer Thompson, raised their glasses and toasted. "To Mickey and Tommy Dorsey, forever number one, always in our hearts, we will be seeing you whenever this song plays." A great cheer erupted from the bar.

Throughout *The Dublin Rogue*, tiny groups laughed as they shared their favorite Mickey stories. One by one, people made their way to the booth in the back to give Henry their condolences.

Luna and Sylvia listened as Henry and Mike told their most loved stories of Mickey. Much as everyone was filled with sorrow, it was impossible to feel sad when remembering such a wonderful and full life.

Mickey had a sense of humor few could top. First and foremost, he always thought about the story, and often did things because it would make the tale more fun to tell. After one particularly funny story, as the laughter died down, Henry took a drink of his beer. There was a silence, which needed filling.

"I think Mickey would have liked the party you threw in his honor. The food, picture, and beer are perfect." He looked at Luna, then Sylvia and Mike. "It's perfect."

Luna grabbed Henry's hand. "I'm sorry I never got to meet him. He sounds like the most wonderful man."

* * *

Katarina had not come with Henry but had taken a cab from Brooklyn. Earlier in the day, she had gathered her belongings from the hotel and settled into Henry's place. Kat, wearing black, made her way through the crowd. She came up behind the booth and saw Luna's hand on Henry's. She put her hand on Henry's shoulder and leaned down, giving him a kiss on the cheek. "I am so sorry, Henry. Mickey was always kind to me. He will be missed."

Luna's eyes flashed. Henry stood up from the booth and introduced Katarina to everyone. When she had a chair, Henry slid back into the booth next to Luna. The tension was slight but unmistakable.

Mike told a story about the time Mickey had hit two trifectas at Aqueduct, went on a whiskey binge, and basically got abducted by circus folk. "The best part was that he woke up three days later, passed out in the clown car. He was wearing floppy shoes and a red nose. Henry had to drive to West Virginia to retrieve him. Not only had he been adopted by the clowns, they had convinced him to join their troop!"

Henry, laughing so hard he was crying, said, "When I arrived, the conjoined twins were begging him to stay, and the midget clown, she was sobbing. They let him keep the nose. He wore it to the bar that night."

The story broke the tension. "I should probably try to find out where his clown friends are, and let them know of Mickey's passing." There were nods and then the sadness was back.

The police chief stopped in, as did the mayor, Robert Wagner. When it was time to close down, the honorable Mayor Wagner issued a "royal decree" extending the hours, which made everyone howl. He had gotten there late, and thought another hour or so would help him with the grieving process. He also bought a round and earned a few votes that night.

When the final toast was done, Mickey's friends gave his picture one last look and headed out. Mike saw to it that Sylvia and Luna made it home, while Henry and Katarina stayed in town, at his apartment. Katarina went to bed, while Henry sat at the kitchen table. His bottle of vodka was ready, but unopened.

Chapter Forty-One

Well past 1:00 a.m., the staff was still on alert. Another full day of Garneau's fury had worn everyone to the breaking point. Everyone except Arthur. He stood in the private viewing room with his employer, sipped brandy, and listened. He didn't mind the endless rehashing of what might or might not happen to the auction. Arthur was not the least bit concerned for the welfare of the other worker bees. He considered himself above the fray. He also saw the advantage in their hatred, in their reaching the boiling point. Their frazzled nerves, the tension in the house, seemed to dovetail nicely with Arthur's own plans.

"It's simply maddening! I have been there since day one. Who does he think he is?" Andre said with a suppressed rage, like a kettle about to blow.

Though rhetorical, Arthur took delight in responding, "He thinks you are a customer, nothing more, nothing less."

This comment had an equal chance of sending his boss into a rage. Arthur was quite content to take some abuse for the good of the team. In fact, he looked forward to it. Instead, Andre simply set his glass down. In a defeated tone, he said, "You might be right. I suppose he does."

Well, everything can't go as planned, Arthur thought.

There was a long silence, the first in two days. The giant of a man stood and walked slowly among his treasures, running his hand over the base of a Degas, "Little Dancer of Fourteen Years," careful not to touch the brass. He stood and looked at it, bending slightly to examine the form more closely. "This was my first love you know," he said, barely audible.

"Sir?"

"I didn't know I liked art, but the money was piling up, and I needed to spend it. I was younger. I saw this in a gallery, in Paris. The tiny dancing girl reminded me of a show my sister was in when we were young. Mother and Father forced me to go, to support her, and I thought it would be boring. I think it was April or May, I don't remember. I just know that my friends…I had friends back then…" His voice faded, he slumped down in his chair and looked at the statue.

Arthur said nothing.

Andre continued. "My friends were heading out somewhere…it was warm and beautiful, but I couldn't go. I was furious. Missing the fun to go watch a ballet was unacceptable, in my mind. So there I was, in the third row, between my parents, watching my sister, in her tutu, dance.

"She was really good. I was shocked. It was the first time I had noticed that she was, well, not my bratty sister." There was another pause.

Arthur couldn't remember if he knew his boss had a sister. He had never thought of him as having had parents, or a childhood, or really anything that might be considered human. "It sounds like you have a lovely sister."

There was another heavy sigh. "Yes…yes I did. When the performance was over, I was the loudest one cheering. I was so proud of her, and I made a scene. My parents let me, and she just glowed. We went out and celebrated that night. I don't think I teased her much after that. We became close, and I didn't even mind when she wanted to tag along that summer. She went to the lake with my friends and me, we swam, and they even grew to like her. She got small pox that winter and died. My parents shipped me off to boarding school, as they were overcome with grief. I've been an ass ever since."

Arthur felt uncomfortable with this display of humanity.

Andre turned back to the statue. "I saw this and thought of her. It was my first piece of art. I don't know when it went from buying something beautiful because it made me happy, to hoarding and hiding away such great works out of spite."

Arthur was perplexed, and his usual poker face failed him.

"I know my friend…I know. I am just so tired. I have been screaming and yelling for days, or is it years? I don't know. The latter, I guess; all my adult life, really. I am an angry, bitter, fat, old man. Why do I care so much about some two thousand year old contraption?"

Arthur had to use his deft touch; he sensed Andre going off script. This wouldn't do. He needed to press just the right button. "You care, because 'The Falcon' cares, and because this time, you will win and show the bastard who is…" he paused briefly for effect, "…king!"

Andre said nothing.

Arthur stood up. "Boss, don't let me hear you talking like this. We have worked too hard and are far too close. It will be the crown jewel in one of the finest collections ever amassed. It will be your legacy."

There was a slight spark behind the defeated eyes. "Arthur, you have been a dear friend. I know you are right. I don't know where my head was, but tomorrow we will continue on. As you said, we are too close to let that bastard, Falcon, best us, again."

There wasn't the same fire in his words, but at least he wasn't giving up. Arthur didn't need him for much longer.

Andre walked out of the study and made his way up to his room.

The upstairs maid, sleeping in a chair in the corner, still wearing her ridiculous uniform, stood at attention when she heard his heavy feet climbing the stairs. "Shall I get your robe, *monsieur?*"

"Yes, please." He followed her into the bedroom. She helped him off with his dinner jacket, then he said, "I will be fine. You may go."

"*Oui monsieur*, are you sure? I haven't gotten your robe."

"It is fine. I am done torturing you for the day. In fact, I have been just horrible to you and the others. I am sorry. Tomorrow, I will make amends."

The stunned look on her face and the gawking silence, when she opened her mouth, would have normally caused an outburst, but Andre said, "It's okay, I know, I am not my normal self. But maybe that is a good thing. My normal self isn't very nice. I'll see you in the morning. Please, tell everyone they can go to bed, and that we should all sleep in a little tomorrow."

She backed out of the room with a simple, "*Oui.*"

The rest of the staff, except for Arthur, was in various states of slumber around the kitchen table. When she told them what he had said, there was a collective look of disbelief. There was also a general feeling of relief that the storm had passed. They all said good night to one another and went off to their rooms, each wondering what tomorrow would bring. None of them would guess what was in store.

Chapter Forty-Two

Henry, lying on his side, opened his eyes with great effort. The room was filling with a new day's light, and it stung. The watch on the nightstand appeared a bit blurry, but seemed to indicate it was after 7:00 a.m. Henry rolled to his back and noticed he was alone. It was curious that Katarina should be up so early. He hoped she was making coffee. A deep breath told him she wasn't. He reached over to the other side of the bed; it was still warm. She hadn't been gone long – always the detective.

Henry could sense his brain moving, but just barely. He listened to the noise of the city, sure that the pounding drum beat was just for him. His hangover lacked rhythm. The bed was warm – that, he was sure of – but the world outside still seemed cold. He missed his friend.

A little chuckle snuck out as he lay there recalling the stories from the wake. Mickey would have loved it, as he always enjoyed a reason to drink and tell stories. He thought about how Mickey would be further along with the case. There was a honking horn, then another. *Yellow Cabs*, thought Henry.

He flipped off the covers and swung his legs out of bed. Running his hands through his hair and over his face, Henry made a quick mental checklist. Shower, coffee, eat, more coffee, go to work, repeat steps two through four. He needed to dig into the names on the list. Who was this "Falcon"? Henry made his way to the shower, turned on the cold, and pulled his body into the shocking water. It helped. Henry was just buttoning up his shirt when the phone rang.

"Hello."

"Henry, I am sorry for calling so early, but it's important."

"It is okay, Professor, what have you got?"

"I spent the day deep in the bowels of the library yesterday. I found nothing. Not even a whiff of mention of the Eye of God. My skepticism grew considerably, so I called a friend at Oxford. I couldn't find anything about another Antikythera mechanism, so I thought I would see if I could dig up something on this mysterious group who found and protects it. My friend is an expert on secret societies like the Ordo Templi Orientis…"

The fog was slowly lifting. "The what?"

"The Ordo Templi Orientis is a mysterious group which started in the 12th century, but that isn't important. I was saying that there are lots of groups – The Freemasons, The Black Hand, and even The Thule Society – which had in their membership Rudolf Hess, Arthur Rosenberg, and it is rumored, Hitler. So, I asked him if he knew of a relatively new group in Greece, protecting some artifact. I was careful and tried to speak only in broad terms."

"He said he didn't know of any such group, as he is focused on groups from the 15th century. I hope you don't mind, but I decided to ask if he knew anything of the Antikythera mechanism. He did and became very excited. His interest was piqued, so I explained that I was doing research on a rumored second device, and was trying to track down the name of the group in Greece who has it. To say he was enthusiastic would be an understatement. I explained the importance of keeping it secret, at least until I publish my findings. I also promised to give him a credit, if he could dig up the name of the group."

"Publish your findings?"

"Don't worry, I'm not going to publish anything, but it's how we in the world of academia work; our life blood, if you will. 'Publish or perish' is the old saying. Anyway, he said he was happy to do some checking and that he'd get back to me in a few days. I couldn't think of a reason to ask for it more quickly, so I left it at that."

"There must be more to the story. I can tell you're setting me up for a dramatic conclusion."

Professor Brookert laughed. "I do try to have a flair for the dramatic. Yes, he called back this morning. He was almost unable to contain himself. Apparently, there was a group called The Thorstians which was mostly disbanded during the War. He wasn't sure how many members there were, but apparently their numbers were greatly depleted during the fighting. The few that remained failed to keep the artifact safe, as it was stolen by the Nazis in 1944. Or that was the rumor. He found an article in an obscure Greek underground newspaper which questioned whether it had been truly stolen by Nazis or perhaps it was just a couple of opportunistic Thorstians who weren't as loyal as the others. It seems it was a paper for members of the club."

"That is interesting, but…"

"Oh, I'm not done. It appears the paper is still around, though it has grown beyond the business of the Thorstians, and my friend was able to talk to the editor, who was there when it happened. He didn't have many details beyond the article, but he did say that there were still those who believed they had been betrayed. It was also rumored that the remaining Thorstians had an idea who it might be and had vowed to see them dead and to do anything to get their treasure back. My friend found the name in an old newspaper article 'Eye of God' and got a description. He says it sounds very similar to the Antikythera mechanism, but that the Eye of God was in working condition, though the editor didn't think it really did anything. I trust my friend, but I may have opened a can of worms by letting him in on our secret. I am going to need to come up with a reason for giving up on the research."

"You made the right move. This is exactly what our client wants to know. It will help justify our fee and keep him happy while I continue to look for Mickey's killer. Oh, and that reminds me, I meant to call you yesterday. Don't take this the wrong way, but I asked another friend to look into it as well."

"Really? You doubted me." He sounded a little hurt, but mostly curious.

"His name is Bobby. He's a strange little guy who rented me my current office. He wanted to help on the case, so I thought I would throw him a bone. I don't expect him to have any luck, but I wanted you to know. He is an annoying little fellow, but is starting to grow on me."

"You are a kind man, Henry Wood. I'd like to meet Bobby, and I'll bring him up to speed on what I've found. Make him feel like part of the team."

"You're aces, Prof. Pop by the office later, and I'll introduce you."

Henry almost made a call to Dr. Schaeffer, but thought better of it. It was still pretty early, so it could wait. Starting off the day with a little good news helped his hangover.

Chapter Forty-Three

Patrick had been filling boxes for a couple of hours. The radio's volume was barely audible, not much more than white noise. Humming to himself, he applied the packing tape. He had done a lot of soul searching and was at peace with his decision to get out of the business. Maybe he would try painting something not painted before or…perhaps not. It might be nice just to sleep, drink, and wile away the hours.

The phone, under a box, gave a muted ring.

"Yes?"

"I have the final location finished. When will the showings begin?"

"I'll have a schedule delivered to you tomorrow."

There was a click on the other end, which Patrick liked. Short, to the point, and once the question was answered, done. He continued to pack as he thought about how he would word the invites for the viewing. Short and sweet, a quick review of the process, though it wasn't necessary, as they had all been through his auctions. He would start with Dr. Schaeffer, as he was always polite, which Patrick appreciated. Then he would invite Andre Garneau, who was seldom polite, usually annoying, and such a pain, he wanted to get him out of the way. Mr. Brown, sadly, had passed.

The phone rang again. A thick accent, speaking too quickly for Patrick to understand, was shouting at him.

"Who is this, and what do you want?"

"We want what is ours," the voice said more clearly. Then the line clicked off.

Patrick sat down. This was upsetting. In all his years, he had never had one of his deals go south. Too much was getting out of control. Patrick didn't like this at all. *How in the hell has anyone gotten this number?* he thought. He spent a few minutes trying to figure out how many times he had given it out. Six times, all to people he trusted. He stopped packing. He could send for the stuff later. Patrick put on his collar and headed off to the church. Paranoia began its assault on his calm.

* * *

Celine had the office open, and Henry noticed a new plant.

"That is a nice touch. What kind is it?"

"It is the green kind."

"You don't know?"

"I liked the shape of the leaves and thought it would look good in the corner, which it does. I have named it 'Betty.' She is a friendly plant."

"Is she?"

"Yes, in fact, I believe she will be an excellent guard plant."

Henry sensing that this could go on for a while, said, "Any messages?"

"Yes, the professor is on his way, as is Mike. Bobby called too; he is very excited. He found something out, but was talking too quickly for me to understand what. I imagine he may have had a stroke, so I don't expect we will see him. I hope not, but he was pretty wound up."

"He will be fine. It's his way."

Henry grabbed a cup of coffee. He placed a call to update Dr.

Schafer, who was pleased to hear from him. Then he dug out Mickey's notebook and recopied the pages he had given the captain, in his own notebook. It was still troubling Henry that he couldn't decipher Mickey's code.

The phone rang and Celine answered it. Henry was pleased with his hire. He heard her answering a few questions; it was obviously a wife looking to catch her husband. She told her they were booked, but could set up an appointment for next week.

He turned back to his deciphering and noticed the words seemed to have fewer vowels than he would have expected. He remembered a time, when they were both drunk. Mickey had made a toast, "To words with no vowels." Henry thought it was one of the funniest things he had ever heard. Now there were a bunch of words without vowels, but they weren't really words at all. Henry counted the number of letters in each group, but that didn't get him anywhere. Maybe each letter equaled a numeric, he thought to himself.

Henry wasn't sure, but his gut told him he was on the right track. The phone rang again. He ignored it until Celine said, "Mr. Wood, a woman named Luna, for you."

"Hey Luna, how are you feeling today?"

She laughed. "I took the day off from the bakery. I am feeling a little rough."

"Me too, but I owe Mickey, so I drug myself out of bed."

A heavy sigh came, then, "I feel just terrible about Mickey, even though I never met him. After hearing the stories last night, I know I would have liked him a lot."

"You did a good job with the wake. Mickey would have loved it. I like to think he was watching."

"So you made it home all right…er…obviously, I guess."

Henry sensed the question not being asked, but didn't want to discuss it. "Yes."

"Good, well, I just wanted to make sure you were okay. I will let you get back to work. If you need anything, don't hesitate to ask."

"Thanks Luna, you are a good friend."

The sound of Bobby coming was unmistakable. The decoding would have to wait.

Chapter Forty-Four

Bobby shut the door, louder than he intended. "Sorry." He opened it up again, peeked through at Celine, then whispered, "Sorry, I didn't mean to slam the door."

Celine giggled.

"Henry, I have a friend, well, really more of an acquaintance. He lives in London, drinks too much, but he's really smart. He used to work for a guy who was some professor at Oxford. You know, tweed suits, proper accent, snooty attitude.... Well, I met the professor once. It was a few years ago..." He took a breath and looked up at the ceiling. "...no, I think it has been almost ten years ago...wait, it was before the war. It was a long time ago. I didn't think he would remember me, so I called Norton. Norton is my friend, well, acquaintance. I like him well enough; I suppose we could be friends. It is hard though, him living in London and all."

Henry listened. Bobby seemed to be on a roll, and disrupting his runaway train of thought could be dangerous. It wasn't worth the risk.

"So I called Norton yesterday. He was pleased to hear from me. It was late afternoon, so he had a few pints in him, but he could still talk. Sometimes he can't, he gets drunk and his accent is so thick I can't make out a word. I asked him if he knew if the guy he worked for at Oxford was still there teaching. He said, 'No, he is here drinking.' He then went on to tell me a lengthy story of how the professor got kicked out for a transgression with a grad student. He said it was rather unseemly and rather funny. I could tell you the story, but I am sure you want me to get to the point."

"I think that boat has sailed."

"Boat? Oh, you mean ship. Yes, you are right, the ship sailed a few weeks ago."

Bobby didn't catch the joke, which made it all the funnier to Henry, but he controlled his smile. "I fear you have lost me. Could you back up to the professor?"

"Oh yes, well, the professor got on the phone and he remembered me, called me a good American chap. He is really quite nice. I feel bad that he lost his job. I asked him if he knew anything about secret societies and ancient artifacts. Could I have some coffee?"

Henry stood up. "Please keep going, I'll get you a cup." Henry poured a cup while Bobby talked at a blistering pace.

"He said he knew everything about secret societies and ancient artifacts. I think this was a bit of a boast, and it was obvious he had a few pints in him as well, but I believe he knows a lot. I had written down the name of the device. I don't remember it now, weird name, but he knew it. As soon as I asked about the anti-thingy, he said he knew of it, but also knew something else. He said it was something nobody knew. Then he ordered another beer. I didn't think it would help, but what could I do?"

Henry handed Bobby the cup of coffee. Bobby took a breath and a sip. "You got any sugar?" Henry handed him the sugar and a spoon. "Okay, where was I? Oh yes...so I asked him what the thing was that nobody knew, and he said there was a secret society, which had almost disappeared during the war, but there were rumors they had survived. I didn't know what he was talking about, but he kept going. They are called the 'Thorstians,' and they are from Greece. I remembered their name, because I knew it was important."

Henry was surprised that Bobby could get so far, and though he already knew about the Thorstians, he flipped open his notebook and wrote it down. Bobby spelled it for him. "Good find, Bobby."

"Oh, that isn't all. The professor went on to tell me that they had their own anti-thingy, but it was much better, and had strange powers."

"What sort of powers?"

"The members of the Thorstians had used it to bring good fortune to their friends and great tragedy to their enemies. He said it didn't always work, and there were times it backfired, but eventually they figured out how to read the dials. Once they understood when it could be used, they were able to find answers to questions, and from there profit greatly. One member had a maritime insurance business, and he would ask if a ship he was considering insuring was doomed. In the first year, he turned away five contracts, and all five ships sank. All of the ships he wrote that year sailed without incident. He told another story of a member who used it to find the woman he was to marry. He had lots of other crazy stories, but at the end, he told me it had been stolen during the war. Not by the Nazis or something, but by a handful of the members, who had taken it and seemingly disappeared. He said the item is priceless, even if the stories about its powers aren't real. He also said it could become invisible. I didn't believe that last part. This is really good coffee."

Henry was now writing furiously. This might explain why some would kill for it. *People have killed for less,* he thought.

"The weird part was this: he knew that the Thorstians had recently discovered that the artifact was heading to New York, to be sold in some secret auction. He also said that the Thorstians almost had the culprits, but that they slipped through their fingers. Now they are in NY, trying to find out about the auction. I asked how he found out this last bit, but a song broke out in the pub, and he was gone. Norton got back on the phone, and we talked a little bit more, but I never got to speak with the professor again."

Henry was writing intently and didn't even notice that Bobby had left. He was in the waiting room telling Celine the same story. Henry thought he heard him jumping with excitement. Celine could be heard encouraging him to "go on."

Henry took a sip of his own coffee and started to reach for the phone, though it wasn't ringing yet. Just then, it did, and he grabbed it before Celine could. "I got it. Hello."

"It's Mike. A buddy called...they fished two Greek guys out of the Hudson. My gut tells me you should get down there and check it out."

Chapter Forty-Five

Father Patrick wasn't much into religion before he donned his collar, but he didn't mind his cover. He liked the church; he enjoyed working with the elderly and hearing confession. His favorite part was the quiet, closely followed by the sound of a choir practicing to an empty room. He often spent hours sitting in the back of the church, listening with his eyes closed. Today a group of men were singing some sort of Gregorian chant. It was delightful; he would have listened, but had too much to do.

As he walked to his office, Patrick sensed people shifting their gaze. The greetings were muted. The little voice in his head was issuing warnings. Patrick knew better than to tune out the little voice. He opened his office door.

"Your Excellence, to what do I owe the pleasure?" Patrick noticed that the bishop wasn't alone, and he gave a quick look to the three priests huddling in the corner.

The bishop remained sitting behind Patrick's desk, his hands folded in his lap, and a look of sadness on his face. "We received a disturbing call, and we would like to hear your side of the story."

"I am sorry, but I don't understand?"

One of the priests began to speak, but a look from the bishop stopped him. "You have been accused of being a fraud." The bishop paused to gauge Patrick's reaction.

Patrick's mind calculated the best expression and tone. "A fraud? By whom?" The tone was a mix of mostly hurt and a small measure of confusion. The confusion was mostly through his facial expression. It was brilliantly delivered.

"The who isn't important, but we must take any accusation seriously, so I have come to talk to you myself. You have, in your time here, done a remarkable job." He looked at the three priests, who all nodded in agreement. "We put in a call to seminary, and they confirmed that you, or at least your name, was there when you said."

Sensing the other shoe was about to fall, he asked, still sounding hurt, "Then what is the problem?"

"I spoke with a priest who thinks he remembers you, but he describes a different man, shorter, much heavier, and bald. I asked him if he was sure, and he said he wasn't. So we need to look into this further."

"Short and fat, hmmm, and balding..." Patrick was talking but really just stalling as he decided on his next move. "I don't know why he wouldn't remember me, but I guess I was pretty quiet, kept to myself."

"He is getting on in years, so it is possibly an honest mistake. What I am wondering though, is why someone felt compelled to level the accusation in the first place. Have you upset someone recently? Do you have any idea why he might have brought this to me?"

Patrick sensed that the scales were tilting in his favor. The bishop was now leaning back in the chair. He seemed more relaxed. It seemed like he was on his side now.

"I really couldn't say. I take confession, help with the food kitchen, and visit some of our older parishioners. There are some people who get upset in the food lines, but when they get full bellies, they calm right down. If I could just talk to the person and ask them, I am sure we could get to the bottom of this."

The bishop shook his head and then stood. He walked over to Patrick and put his hand on his shoulder. "We need to be careful and get to the bottom of this. Even a rumor could be disastrous. We must use caution. This is a serious accusation. It is a crime, but the church would like to keep this in house, while we sort this mess out."

He then did something Patrick didn't expect. He returned to the chair behind the desk and asked the other priests to leave. When the door closed, he leaned forward and looked Patrick in the eye.

"Are you a priest?"

The tone was strong.

Patrick felt like he was a child again, being interrogated by his father. His chest tighten, his mouth went dry, and he wasn't sure if it was showing on his face. The voice was crystal clear: he needed to get out of there, and he needed to leave now. He needed to stare the bishop in the eye and lie to him. He had a lifetime of lying, and he was good at it, but this time was different. It was wrong. He liked the bishop, he liked the other priests, and he couldn't remember ever being happier than he had been pretending to be a priest. He was actually good at it. Not as good as he was at painting forgeries, nor as good as he was at selling stolen art, but he was good. Did he need redemption? It crossed his mind.

Then it was time to answer.

"Yes I am," he said looking down, then looking back up and squarely in the eye of the bishop. "And I can prove it! I have a photo from the seminary. I am younger, but I have my hair, and it is a good photo."

The tone went from sad to excited, and the bishop bought it. "I am glad. I will need to see it."

Patrick hopped up from his chair. "I know exactly where it is. I have an old box...but you don't care about that. If Your Excellency would like, I can run and get it now."

"I think it would be best. I will be pleased to put this whole unpleasant affair behind us."

Patrick walked out of the church and down the street and turned the corner. He passed a bakery, a florist, and a bank, then turned down an alley and tossed his collar into a trash dumpster.

His life in the church was over; soon his days in America would end, too. It would be good to retire, but he didn't feel happy. Should he just walk away from this last deal? No, it will be his greatest triumph. Time would heal the guilt.

Chapter Forty-Six

Hans sat with his legs casually crossed, *The New York Times* in one hand, while his other rhythmically stirred his coffee in its fine china cup. He liked the sound of the bone china. Three taps of the spoon signaled he was done with his routine. Arthur was now acknowledged.

Arthur was a patient man, and familiar with Hans' ways. It was his attention to detail which made Arthur trust him.

"I want to…" Arthur paused when the young woman asked if he would like to order. She smiled when he declined, and went to help another table. "Everything seems to be on schedule."

"Yes, the only three serious bidders who remain are our guys and the Falcon. The bidding should be competitive." Hans set his paper down and sipped his coffee.

"Have you spoken with the Falcon?"

"Yes. I was told to give you kudos on your exemplary service."

"It has been a good run. It will be sad to see it come to an end," Arthur said with a hint of a smile as he took a sip of water.

Hans didn't harbor the same ill feelings towards the Falcon. Hans had his own grudge, his own reason for the betrayal. It wasn't his nature to do anything but follow orders; though he had the mind for being a leader, he preferred to help others run the show. With

Arthur though, they worked well together and contributed equally. Each of them seemed to be able to add key elements to their plan without stepping on one another's toes.

"It has been a good run. I won't miss it, though. I plan to spend the remainder of my days answering to only myself. It will be nice."

"You will go back to Nuremberg?"

"I was thinking Vienna. Am I too old to learn to play the piano?"

Arthur laughed. "I would expect you would be a great pianist."

"Did you learn anything new about the detective? Is he going to be a problem?"

"He is chasing his tail. I don't think he has a clue who the Falcon is, and that is all that matters."

"What about the guys working with him? Mike and the professor."

"Mike is a beat cop. He is taking time off to help his friend investigate Mickey's murder. The professor is some art teacher at NYU and likes to drink. It's possible Wood may figure out that Father Patrick is behind the auctions, but that's his problem, not ours."

The waitress seated an older couple at the table next to theirs, so they stopped talking business and instead discussed their plans for the future, all the dreams they had both been keeping hidden away.

Chapter Forty-Seven

Mike got himself a cup of coffee.

They had just returned from the crime scene, where two Greek men had been found dead. In an alley, about three blocks from the docks, they were stabbed multiple times. They each had their watches, billfolds, and envelopes packed with hundred dollar bills. One didn't need to be Sherlock Holmes to know it wasn't a robbery. A patrolman found a sailor who knew who they were and that they had come in on a ship called *The Siena*.

Mike and Henry had the patrolman take them to find the sailor, and learned that the two men had traveled not as crew, but as guards for a large box. They never left its side, even when the weather got really rough. He didn't know what was in the box, but he overheard the two men saying they thought it was cursed. They also found out that the ship had arrived the previous night.

The area the men were found in had quite a few bars. Both men reeked of alcohol, so Mike guessed there could be a waitress or bartender who might remember two drunk Greeks. It was too early for any of them to be open, so they went back to the office with plans to canvas the neighborhood later in the day.

"What's the plan?" Mike asked.

Henry made a slight grunting noise. "I assume you are using the term 'plan' in the loosest possible sense."

"I was."

This made Henry smile. "This Andre Garneau person is another collector. I thought we should pop over to his house and try to get an audience with him."

"You make him sound like royalty."

"Remember when I told you about my visit to the Matisse gallery?"

"Yeah, I remember...oh, that's right, you saw him there."

"He was hard to miss. Mostly though, I heard him and how he talked to the owner. It was condescending, bordering on rude, and completely elitist."

"That sounds like every rich guy I ever met."

"How many rich guys you ever met?"

"I know the mayor and..."

"The mayor didn't seem too elitist when he was pouring you a beer last night."

"Well...I have run into a few like Garneau, but you are right, the mayor is a good guy. So we gonna go rattle his cage?"

"I thought we might try a two-pronged attack. I'll get in to see him, and you hang outside to see if you can get the inside scoop from his driver."

"Sounds good to me...I bet I find out more than you do."

"It's a bet...lunch?"

There was a slightest tinge of pain, as Henry remembered all the bets he and Mickey had made, but he quickly got over it. "There's one more thing. I want you to drive, let me out, and then park the car. My gut tells me there has been someone keeping an eye on what we are doing, but I haven't seen anyone."

"You want me to be your driver?" Mike said, raising an eyebrow.

"Yes."

Mike didn't laugh as often as Henry, or most people, but when he did, it was a hearty chortle, to say the least. "I should probably call the captain and let him know we are going to canvas the bars later. He will appreciate us saving him some man hours, and the cooperation will win us a few points. Also, even though we don't have any proof of a connection, he should know we suspect that those murders are tied into this whole art mess."

"That is a good call...pun intended."

Henry wandered out into Celine's domain. "How is it going?"

"Everything is running like a well-oiled gazelle."

"Mixing up your metaphors?"

"Not mixing up, mixing, with a giant verbal egg beater." She made a little egg beater motion.

Henry really liked her. "I guess what I meant to say is, well, I haven't given you much to do, but it looks like you have gotten the files in shape, made the office look like it has a tenant, and generally got it..."

"Oily gazelle...I know."

"Exactly! When I find Mickey's killer and we wrap up this case, we can sit down and figure out your official duties."

She went to the filing cabinet, took out a plain manila folder, and handed it to Henry. The heading on the tab was "Celine's Duties." Henry found a neatly typed list of daily duties under the heading "Maintenance," which included opening the office, watering the plant, making coffee, typing up case notes from the previous day, and logging calls.

"We have a call log?"

She handed him another folder.

"This is impressive. I am going to be able to handle a lot more..." Henry was handed another folder with the heading "Prospective Clients."

"There have been three people who have inquired about your services. I took their contact information, got a preliminary description of the type of case, and explained that we would call them as soon as the current case was completed. I hope you don't mind me doing this?" she said, genuinely sounding as if she was worried that a boundary had been crossed.

"The only thing I mind is you using 'your,' not 'our' services. How is petty cash holding out?"

"It is fine, though I did spend quite a lot on supplies, and the plant."

"How is Betty doing?"

Celine's eyes lit up. She clapped her hands together three times quickly. "You remembered! She is well. In fact, we just had our daily coffee and water break."

"Does Betty take cream in her coffee?"

Celine liked this comment too, but wasn't about to show it. "Yes she does, and two lumps."

Henry took out a twenty and gave it to Celine. "For the petty cash. Buy whatever you or Betty need."

Henry could tell Celine loved her new job, and the office plant. It was a much friendlier environment than she had working for Mr. Grabby Hands.

Mike came out of the back with his coffee cup. "I told the captain about our morning. He was pleased to get updated. Great coffee, Celine. Where can I rinse out the cup?"

Celine liked that he asked, but took the cup from him. "Don't you worry about it."

Henry handed Mike the keys, and they were off.

Chapter Forty-Eight

The door opened and Henry saw a maid, who was giggling. She wore a conservative long skirt, had her hair neatly pulled back in a bun, and had on sensible shoes. She asked who was calling, then Henry heard a voice coming from deep inside the house.

"Show them in, bring them back here."

Henry followed her back to the kitchen. Sitting at and on the table, a man who looked like a cook and several other staff members were drinking wine. A very large man in a smock of sorts was stirring something in a stock pot. Henry wasn't sure what was going on, so he stood in the doorway. The man turned around.

"Hello, welcome to my home. We are having a celebration of sorts. Glass of wine?"

"No thanks. I'm Henry Wood. I was wondering if I could ask you a few questions."

Andre shook Henry's hand. "I am pleased to meet you. Ask away. Do you mind if I keep an eye on my broth?"

"No, not at all, it smells great."

Andre waved his hand towards the counter on the other side of the massive kitchen. "If not wine, may I offer you some strudel? It is wonderful and freshly made."

Henry noticed the cook grinning ear to ear, and then the maid said, "The best strudel you have ever tasted." She kissed the old cook on the top of his bald head.

"What are you celebrating, and yes, I would love some strudel."

The other maid cut him a piece, put it on a plate, and then got a glass of milk.

"Mr. Wood, we are celebrating a birthday of sorts. Today I have stopped being the complete ass everyone who has ever met me has known and loathed. I reached a pinnacle of meanness over the last few days, as my staff will attest."

They all nodded, and the cook said, "Yes, but you made amends and all is forgiven."

The maid who had answered the door bounced over to Henry and showed him a check. "He gave us all a pay raise, apologized, and then gave us each a bonus. I also got a new uniform." She spun around to show Henry. "It is much nicer."

Andre Garneau said, "I used to make her wear the most dreadful outfit…let's just say that she endured my old lecherous ways for far too long. You see, Mr. Wood, somewhere along the line, I became a monster. My staff has suffered for a long time. Their years of loyalty, quiet suffering, and exemplary service should be rewarded. I am going to enjoy life, but not at the expense of others." He tasted the soup and added more salt.

"May I ask what brought about this epiphany?"

"You certainly may, and what's more, I will be happy to tell you. I collect art, or should I say, I obsess about art. There is an auction coming up, and I coveted the item so much it drove me to the brink of madness. Last night I realized that even if I won the auction, the happiness I would feel would be hollow and meaningless. I can take far more joy in cooking than I ever could sitting alone in a room admiring my collection."

"What were you going to bid on?"

"It was an ancient machine, which supposedly could calculate the position of stars, and was in complete working order. It was over 2,000 years old and supposedly had been perfectly preserved. It would have been the crown jewel of my collection, that is, until I decided I didn't want it anymore."

The chauffeur walked in and said hello, grabbing a piece of strudel. "Hey, I am Claude."

"Henry. Pleased to meet you. What do you do?" Henry asked, already knowing.

"I am Mr. Garneau's driver."

Henry took another bite. "The strudel is really remarkable, my compliments to the chef. So you aren't going to the auction?"

"Nope, and what's more, I am going to sell most of my collection, all the pieces which I bought merely for the lust of collecting. There are some which have meaning, and those I will treasure. May I ask you a question?"

"It seems only fair."

"Mr. Wood, are you the person hired to figure out who is coming to the auction?"

Henry looked at the jolly man cooking and laughing with his staff and considered giving him a straight answer, but it wasn't how he worked. He had made a promise to a client. It was important. "Actually, I am looking into the murder of the man hired. He was my friend." It was true.

Andre stopped stirring and looked at Henry. The look was genuine and was not the sort of expression worn by a man who ordered a hit.

"I am sorry to hear it. Who was your friend?"

"His name was Michael Thomas Moore. He taught me the trade."

The room became very quiet. Andre pulled out a chair for Henry and then sat down across the corner of the table. "Please, Mr. Wood, ask me anything you need to. I will help you as best I can."

"Who is behind the sale?"

There was a knock at the front door, and the maid hustled out to answer it. Andre looked up. "My, we are receiving a lot of guests today. I am sorry, what did you ask me?"

The maid returned with an envelope and handed it to Garneau.

"I was asking you who is behind the auction?"

"Ah, yes. It will be difficult for you to believe when I tell you." Then he stopped as he read the contents of the envelope, and smiled. "Your timing is extraordinary, Mr. Wood." He handed Henry the invitation. "You may have that, as I have no need of it anymore. Claude, would you please give Arthur a call; let him know that invitation has arrived. Tell him I have decided not to bid."

Henry read the invitation to himself until he got to the signature, simply, "Patrick."

"Is this Father Patrick?"

"Yes it is. He has been posing as a priest for a long time, has quite the operation set up."

"How does it work?"

"The auctions are always run the same way: we have an individual viewing, then the next day we call into a phone number he gives us, and bid."

"Do you know the other bidders?"

"I know of some of them, but not all."

"Do you know someone who goes by the name 'The Falcon'?"

Garneau stiffened for a moment, then let out a deep breath. "That name used to upset me greatly. I have lost many fine works to the Falcon, but now I guess those days are over. I would be lying to say I didn't still feel some animosity, but I am sure those feelings will pass in time."

"Who is the Falcon?"

"I don't know who he is, but he's rich. He has some sort of special arrangement with Father Patrick. I have never even heard his voice. We can hear each other bidding, but the Falcon's bids come in some other way, because Father Patrick always tells us what he has bid."

"Do you think Father Patrick is the Falcon, just trying to goose the bidding?"

"I had considered it, but he has won so many auctions, it didn't make sense. Why would Father Patrick go to such great lengths to hold secret auctions and have half of them ending with the Falcon winning? Where is the profit in that?"

Henry made some notes. "That is a good point." Henry smiled and asked for another piece of strudel.

Chapter Forty-Nine

"He what?!" Hans yelled.

Arthur had to hold the phone away from his ear. "He has given up collecting. I just got a call; he got the notice for the viewing, and had Claude call me to say he wasn't going." Arthur answered with an equal measure of frustration and anger.

"What in the world is going on over there? He was your responsibility."

"Don't try to blame me, there isn't any way I could have seen this coming. He has been yelling and going on for days, screaming at anyone within earshot. He was obsessed."

"Something must have happened."

"He was ranting and suddenly took a look at the little Degas, then told me a story about his kid sister. She died when he was young. The next morning, he is writing checks, apologizing for his behavior, and is suddenly everyone's buddy. It is sickening. I want to kill him more than ever."

"We need to think. Who else is able to bid with the doctor and Falcon?"

There was a long pause. "I know what you are implying." Arthur's short temper was beginning to flare.

"I am not implying anything; we are about to see everything, all the years of waiting on these horrible men, come to naught."

"You know as well as I do that the others aren't in a position financially to push the bids. The lawyer from Staten Island, he will bid first and probably be out, the other guy will make two bids at best. The Falcon, Dr. Schaeffer, and Garneau were to battle, driving the price through the roof and keeping them away for hours."

"The Falcon will be thrilled."

"Dr. Schaeffer will not try to battle the Falcon head to head, and will drop out after it hits five million. We needed Garneau and the mutual hatred between him and Schaeffer to keep the doctor in the mix. I will make the call, let the Falcon know what has happened. I will meet you in an hour. I am not giving up - we just need to calm down and think."

"I will meet you. Oh, and ask if the Falcon has gotten the invite yet."

"One hour."

* * *

Henry got in the car and said, "Sorry, buddy, I thought Claude might be hanging out with the car, but he was inside."

"I figured. I got a cup of coffee and waited. You were in there a long time...learn anything? Is he our guy?"

"My gut tells me no. He had some sort of epiphany and isn't even going to the auction. So we are back at square one."

"My money is on the Falcon. The other two guys on the list were both out of town that night."

"Yeah, and they mostly collect statues. I was sure Dr. Schafer, Garneau, or the Falcon were responsible."

"You might still be right. What did the messenger bring?"

"Oh yeah, I almost forgot. He brought an invitation from Father Patrick. It seems the show is about to begin."

"So your gut was right about the priest. I wonder if our client has his yet."

Henry was thinking the same thing. The traffic was pretty bad and though it wasn't a terribly long drive back to the Flatiron Building, it was going to take a while. Henry wondered what Katarina was doing, as that usually lifted his spirits. The problem was it still seemed like the world was covered in a dark, gray mist. In truth, it was clear out, the sun was shining down on the city, and people were starting to feel the hope of spring to come.

As Mike drove, Henry, not used to being a passenger, looked out the window. He saw a man helping a woman get out of a cab. There was another person opening a door for someone with their arms full of grocery bags. Didn't these people know that a great man had been taken from all of them?

Maybe it wasn't the good deeds or even the loss of Mickey, he thought. Perhaps it was just the way that everything kept going, unabated. If he was honest with himself, he had gone on with his life, chasing a case, being the detective. This thought made it even worse.

He tried to picture Katarina and how she looked last night, but the image wouldn't stay. It was the picture of Mickey on the cold street which kept coming back.

Mike parked the car two blocks away, and they walked towards the office. Leaning against the building, smoking, were Henry's three leather-clad buddies.

"Hey fellas, what brings you around?"

Stan took a drag, trying to look cool, and was about to talk when Lawrence said, "Father Patrick has left. He was accused of being a fake, and bolted."

Henry and Mike looked at each other, then Henry asked, "Who ratted him out?"

"Nobody knows, but the bishop was there, then Patrick left and never came back."

"Good work, boys." Henry handed each of them a twenty and said, "Keep your eyes and ears open. If you find out where he went, let me know."

It was obvious by the looks on their faces that they were pleased to have helped. Henry wasn't comfortable being looked up to, but he could grow to like these three. He and Mike headed upstairs to call the professor, get in touch with Dr. Schaeffer, and to plan the endgame. He couldn't be sure, but Henry's gut told him they were close to finding the killer...or not. Soon the players would be gone. It was now or never.

Chapter Fifty

Sitting in the office were Henry at his desk and the professor in the chair. Mike stood in the corner, drinking some coffee.

"Dr. Schaeffer is picking us up in a few minutes. Mike, you follow us, at a reasonable distance, and then hang out after we leave the viewing. See if you can catch a glimpse of the recently defrocked Father Patrick or anyone who's working with him. Follow them if you can do it without being seen."

"Will do."

Bobby came in with Celine, holding a piece of paper. "Hey guys, how are we doing?"

The professor, who had grown fond of the odd, little man, said, "Bobby, good to see you. Whacha got in your hand there?"

Bobby handed the paper to the professor. "I got a call from my friend who knew a few symbols which could be found on each of the three boxes. He told me the exact book I could find them in, and the pages, and so I went to the library and traced them. I thought you would want these for the viewing."

Mike and Henry looked at each other, smiling, and the professor said, "I can't believe you found this...amazing, and thank you." The professor looked at the paper, studying each symbol closely. "This will really help me sound convincing, which I was concerned about."

Henry took a look at the symbols. "Dr. Schaeffer will be pleased. We should probably head down to the lobby, so as not to keep him waiting."

The sedan pulled up. Hans was driving; Professor Brookert got in the front seat, while Henry joined Dr. Schaeffer in the back. They drove uptown and stopped at a corner, where a man approached and handed a piece of paper to Hans. It had the address of the viewing area. It took forty minutes to make it to the building, in a rather dodgy area. Hans stayed with the car and handed the paper to Dr. Schaeffer.

"It says go to the second floor, down to the end of the hall, and knock on the last door on the left."

"Is this how it always goes?"

"Yes, lots of cloak and dagger stuff, though usually they give us a day's notice, not a few hours."

"I wonder why the short notice?" the professor asked.

The building appeared to be empty, as they didn't run across anyone in the halls or on the stairs. Henry and the professor let Dr. Schaeffer lead the way. He knocked and Patrick opened the door. Their jaws dropped. The room looked like it might be huge, but it was hard to tell, what with all the mirrors.

The doctor said, "You have outdone yourself this time. Though it looks like a carnival fun house, it is impressive nonetheless."

Patrick said, "The credit goes to Randy, as always, but thanks."

Patrick looked unsettled at seeing Henry in tow.

They walked through a lengthy set of mirrored halls and arrived in a circular room with the three boxes set in a triangle. The Eye of God sat atop the smallest of the three.

Dr. Schaeffer looked at the professor, and waved his arm. "Please, Professor Brookert, and take your time."

The professor pulled out a magnifying glass. "May I touch it?", he asked, looking at Patrick.

"You may touch the boxes, but please not the device."

The larger of the boxes was faded and pretty rough, the sea had been hard on it. The professor ran his finger over the carvings and carefully looked at each face of the box, finding the symbol he was looking for on the side. The second box was an entirely different style, but the symbol was there, just as Bobby's friend had said it would be. The third box looked brand new, and on the top in the center, was the design he was looking for, and he turned his attention to the device.

"This is remarkable, completely amazing. I am awestruck."

"So it is your opinion that it is genuine?"

"There is little which is known about this mysterious machine, but I would have to say I don't see any indications that it isn't from the time period suggested. Beyond that, I can't offer much more."

"I appreciate your evaluation. I am satisfied."

Dr. Schaeffer and Henry then took about fifteen minutes to look it over. When they were finished, they walked out of the mirrored room.

The sound of a small bang made them all turn around. The little room had filled with smoke, and when it cleared a few moments later, the boxes and the device were nowhere to be seen.

Patrick simply explained, "Randy is quite a showman."

The ride back to the Flatiron building was full of chatter about the Eye of God. Hans had a lot of questions, and Professor Brookert was happy to share all of the finer points he had noticed. There were symbols, beyond the ones he was looking for, which also helped him determine the age. "I was looking for anything which might be known to be more recent; it all looked authentic."

When they returned to the office, the stories were told again for Celine's and Bobby's benefit. They had talked for almost an hour when Celine suddenly asked about Mike. He was long overdue.

Henry was concerned - it showed on his face - and the room became quiet. Now everyone was worried.

Chapter Fifty-One

Patrick was anxious. He was always in control of his emotions. When he got the polite decline of his invitation from Garneau, after having been caught by the church, he was angry. It had been with him all day. The only thing which calmed him down was the meeting with Dr. Schaeffer and his people. He was glad they were gone now. He wasn't sure how the detective was connected to his client, but he couldn't dwell on that now.

The more he thought about the meeting, the more bothered he became, though. Henry hadn't seemed the least bit surprised at seeing him. Had Henry seen through his priest cover? Could it have been Henry who called the bishop with the accusations? But why would he do that? It didn't make sense. If he was working for Dr. Schaeffer, then he wouldn't want to do something to risk the sale.

Henry was polite when they shook hands. Damn, he had a good poker face.

Maybe Dr. Schaeffer had told him what was up?

That seemed like the most logical conclusion.

He hadn't heard back about the funeral. If Henry knew that his being a priest was a cover, he may have made other arrangements.

These thoughts continued to swirl around in his head, making him more uncomfortable, and he was on the cusp of paranoia. He looked at his watch; there was still fifteen minutes before he was to meet the Falcon.

Patrick started to think about who might have called the bishop. He hadn't seen Stan and his friends in a while; they were supposed to be keeping tabs on Henry. They were just kids though, probably off drinking. He went through the checklist of every person he had in his employ, and none of them seemed likely to have done it. They were all paid very well...what was the upside, what could their angle have been? No, it wasn't one of his people.

He looked around to see if there was anyone watching him. Patrick didn't expect to see anyone, but then again, he was starting to lose it.

Across the street, looking out of a stairway window on the second floor was a large man, keeping an eye on him. Patrick couldn't see him: it was getting dark and there weren't any lights in the hallway. Patrick saw the van pull out of the loading bay and pull up next to him.

"I am off to the second location; I need a couple of hours to set up."

"Thanks, Randy, the mirrors were great. I give you high marks for the flourish at the end."

"I try to be a showman, so you get your money's worth."

"As always, you have earned everything coming to you. Fine work, Randy."

The van drove away and Patrick thought to himself, "Yes, you arrogant little bastard. After all these years and all the money, you still can't follow instructions. It will be a pleasure making you disappear." He felt the Walther PPK in his pocket.

Under the street light, a figure in a dark trench coat and hat lit up a cigarette. It was the signal. Patrick lit up one himself and started to walk. The figure, remaining on the other side of the street, followed. The person in the window quickly made his way down to the street and followed them both. It was tricky, as the point of them walking on opposite sides of the street was to be able to keep an eye open for anything out of the ordinary, but he wasn't noticed.

Patrick was hungry and was pleased the Falcon had chosen a restaurant. Patrick liked the Falcon; he respected the Falcon's organization and skill at keeping secrets. In that, they were birds of a feather. He looked over his shoulder, thinking he had seen something. The paranoia was getting bad. A nice meal would help.

The figure entered the restaurant first, and then Patrick crossed the street. He hungs his coat next to a dark trench coat. On the lapel was a small falcon, *this is the one*, he thinks. Patrick slipped the instructions into the pocket and then asked for a table.

Mike rounded the corner in time to see Patrick enter the restaurant. He crossed to the other side of the street. Mike stood there for a while and then decided to find a pay phone.

"Hey Henry, this is Mike."

Henry said, so everyone could hear him, "Mike, good to hear from you buddy, where are you at?"

"I hung out after you left. It took a little while, but then I saw them load up the van. Your guy Patrick then took to waiting for someone. I found a good vantage point and was able to keep an eye on him. I don't know how long he stood there, maybe 20 – 30 minutes, but eventually they showed up. I couldn't see who it was. I followed them to a restaurant. They're in there now."

"We were getting worried."

Mike chuckled, "Sorry, but I couldn't get to a phone and keep an eye on him."

"Can you get a look inside the restaurant, without being seen?"

"I can, but does it matter? Patrick doesn't know me from Adam."

"It probably doesn't, but I want to play it close to the vest."

"Will do, I'll call in later. Are you going to be at the office?"

"Yes. I'll order some Chinese food and wait for your call."

"Order me some egg rolls and soup."

Mike walked to the corner and crossed, then approached the window. He tried to look casual by reading the menu, when all of a sudden there was a pounding. He looked and Francis LeMange, the food critic and up until recently, someone he didn't care for, was knocking and motioning for him to come inside. When Mike was in the hospital, earlier in the year, Francis came by every day to check on him. Their common friendship with Henry had been enough, their differences had vanished. Now, they were friends and it was biting him right in the butt. It couldn't be avoided.

Mike went in and joined Francis at the table in the window. At least he would be able to eat.

Chapter Fifty-Two

Mike shook Francis's hand and took a seat. The table had a bottle of wine, and Francis had still been looking at the menu when he spotted Mike. He had his notebook out, pen at the ready, and a blank page awaiting his thoughts.

"I'm just delighted that you happened past my little window seat. It will be nice to have someone to dine with this evening."

"Are you here doing a review for the paper?" Mike said looking around the restaurant. He spotted Patrick sitting alone near the far wall.

"*Oui et Non*, I am working on my article, but it isn't about tonight's meal, but today's lunch. I eat here fairly often. The calamari is brilliant." Francis waved his hand and a young man with jet black hair appeared next to the table. "It would bring me an almost immeasurable amount of pleasure to share, with my friend Mike, a plate of your calamari."

The waiter looked at Francis and then Mike. "It will be right up and I'll bring a wine glass for your guest."

"I have to admit I was getting pretty hungry."

"Did you catch any bad guys, today?"

"I decided to take a couple of week's vacation and help Henry on a case. Did you hear about Mickey?"

"No, what happened? I just got back from Lyon last night."

Mike lowered his voice, "He was killed by a hit and run and Henry thinks its murder. He has convinced me, so I took the time off to help." Mike leaned in slightly, "I am sort of working now, so…"

Francis was sharp and whispered, "Play it cool, got it. Normal dinner conversation," and then raising his voice, "The veal is fantastic, but so is the pasta. This place has been here for over 30 years, as has most of the staff, except the young man who helped us. He is new and very eager."

The waiter returned with a glass, poured Mike some wine, and said, "The calamari is on its way. Are you ready to order?"

"I need a few minutes…and a menu." Mike said with a smile.

The waiter blushed, "Of course, I am so sorry." He scurried away and returned almost immediately, then ran off again, likely to hide his shame.

Mike and Francis had a good meal. They talked easily, telling stories and laughing, just like old friends. They were friends, but had mostly just tolerated each other until this year. During the calamari and throughout the entire main course, Patrick never looked over once. He dined alone, which meant that one of the other patrons was the mysterious person in the dark trench coat.

Mike excused himself and went to the men's room. On his way he noticed the black trench coat was still hanging there and when he returned he saw her. Katarina was eating alone at a corner table. As far as he could tell, there were only two people dining alone. Mike may have only been in the detective business for a few days, but he could do the math. He also knew that nobody else on the list was here, so she was somehow mixed up in this mess.

Mike returned to the table and ate slowly, enjoying the food and the company. The waiter returned and asked about dessert. Francis insisted they both try the cheesecake. Mike trusted the food critic's choice. He was glad he had, as it was the best he had ever eaten.

Mike was so enjoying his cheesecake that he didn't notice Katarina approaching. "Mike what are you doing here?"

If she was involved, and was half as clever as Henry said, she would be suspicious. "This is my friend Francis, he and I were just catching up. He is the food critique for the paper. He asked if I wanted to join him for dinner and I have learned never to turn down those invitations. Are you here with Henry?" He stood up and looked around. It worked, now she needed to make an excuse.

"No, he was working late, so I had to eat alone." She donned a pouty face.

Francis leaned forward, "Delighted to meet you…"

"Oh sorry, this is Katarina; she is a friend of Henry's from way back."

Francis smiled and shook her hand.

"It is nice to meet you, too. So how does this place rate?"

Francis didn't know if he should tell the truth about not actually being out reviewing, so he just leaned back, and dabbed his mouth with a napkin. "If you were to guess, based upon my face, what would you say?" He smiled broadly.

"I would say it gets an A. I know I enjoyed myself. Feel free to quote me on that." She spoke easily and with incredible charm. Mike noticed Patrick leaving and when he walked past the window, so did Katarina.

"Would you like to join us for a cup of coffee?" Mike said, suspecting she would decline.

"Thank you, Mike, but I have to be going."

When Katarina walked past the window she gave them a wave. They both waved back. She wore the black trench coat.

Chapter Fifty-Three

The Professor, Bobby, and Henry were eating and listening to Celine tell a story from one summer in the Poconos. Henry had bought take out for everyone. It was a bit of unwinding he sorely needed. Mike walked in just as Celine was saying, "...and though I never found my swimsuit, it was worth it, even though the nickname stuck."

"Henry, could I talk to you outside?"

The ominous tone in his voice made everyone stop eating and look at Mike and then Henry. "Sure Mike, let's take a walk."

As they closed the office door, there was a collective shrug and they heard Celine ask the professor, "So Prof, you ever have a nickname?"

Henry and Mike walked down the hall and stopped at the other end. "What is it Mike?"

"I tried to get a look in the restaurant, but had an unexpected turn."

"Oh?"

"Francis was there, in the window, about to have dinner. He sort of insisted I join him. I don't think Patrick noticed me. He ate alone and I never saw anyone approach his table, aside from the waiter."

"Interesting...but why so secretive?"

"The person in the trench coat, well I didn't see them sit down. I didn't know who it could be, all the other tables were couples or groups, well except one. It was Katarina."

Henry looked out of the window at the end of the hall, then shook his head, and turned back to Mike. "She's the Falcon."

"You knew?!"

"No, but I suspected. I have been avoiding the signs, her returning, our case involving the art underworld, and the way she seemed to to avoid my questions. I let myself get drawn in. Mickey once told me, 'Never let Dames fog your mind.' I didn't listen. But I am now." His voice was low and sad, but resolved. He accepted what he had suspected and was ready to move on.

"Does this mean..."

"I am not ready to jump to that conclusion, but I am prepared for it to be true."

"She isn't working alone."

"I agree. We should bring everyone up to speed." Henry turned and walked back to the office.

When they joined the others the professor had just finished his nickname story. Henry sat down behind his desk. Celine jumped up, "We have saved some for you Mike." Her beaming voice made Henry feel a little less dreadful. "He's eaten. Go ahead, Mike, tell them what you learned." Henry flipped open his notebook.

* * *

Across town Katarina flipped up her collar. She had left her hat at the restaurant, as she figured Mike would find it odd, her wearing a fedora. Another five minutes and Patrick would pick her up for the viewing. She couldn't wait. She believed in the Eye of God, she believed it with every fiber of her being.

Katarina couldn't put into words her love of art. She didn't remember why she had wandered into that museum when she was sixteen. She only remembered how she felt seeing the 19th century

Russian icon, "St. Nicholas —Woodworker". It was a show full of Russian iconography, but this one piece, in the corner, had drawn her in. She stood looking at it for a few minutes, but it must have been hours, because afterwords it was dark outside.

The gallery had been mostly empty when she bought her ticket. A docent at the front desk asked if she wished to have a tour and she had declined, saying she preferred to just look. This one icon stopped her in her tracks and after looking over every detail, she suddenly felt as if she was surrounded by people. She sensed them all about, but was frozen, like in a dream. She tried to break eye contact with St. Nicholas, but could not. She couldn't see anyone in her peripheral vision, but she heard them, talking, filling the room with sound. They spoke in different languages, this crowd, but there was one tongue which seemed clearer than the others. It was Aramaic. She knew it, but didn't know how, as she had never even heard of Aramaic, let alone heard it. Then she heard a voice talking to her, but she couldn't understand the words. The icon let her go, she turned to see the crowd, but was alone. An hour later the fog of time had hidden this memory from her.

It was years later, at a lecture in Syria, she heard a professor read a passage in Aramaic, "The Eye of God can see all and knows when to listen." The professor explained that this meant God was always watching and knew to which prayers he must pay special attention. Katarina knew that his interpretation was mistaken, that it referred to something else entirely, something specific. The fog which had clouded her memory of that day burned away. Suddenly, she remembered all of it, the people, the Russian Icon, and what they were all talking about. It was the Eye of God, and they told her she would find it. She carried this with her, and now, standing on the cold street, she took strength knowing she was on the right path.

A car pulled up. Patrick opened the door and she got in. "Did you enjoy your dinner?"

"I did. And you?"

"It was fine. Randy will take us to his next amazing hiding place."

Randy looked over his shoulder, "It is a ways from here and with the traffic, it will take a while, but soon you will be in the presence of the Eye of God."

She didn't appreciate his cavalier tone. The showmanship seemed to be mocking the sacred treasure. She leaned back and tried to relax, but she was uneasy. She had good reason to be, as they were being followed.

Chapter Fifty-Four

Arthur and Hans pulled away from the curb after Patrick and Katarina and another car drove past. The traffic was typical for that time of night, and they stayed a ways back. Arthur smoking, with one hand on the wheel, "They don't' seem to be in too much of a hurry."

"Just don't get close enough that Patrick notices, he is very careful, but don't lose them either."

Arthur resented the implication that he didn't know how to tail someone. It wasn't the time for a debate with Hans, so he let it go. "So what's the plan for tomorrow?"

Hans rolled down his window, for the fresh air, and said "I have been thinking about that, we may need to move forward without the Garneau collection."

"So I don't get my pound of flesh? Is that what you are suggesting?"

"Your original plan was brilliant, while Garneau, Schafer and the Falcon are bidding, we hit them; you robbing Dr. Schaeffer and me taking Garneau's collection, and then dealing with the Falcon afterward. But if everything you have told me about Garneau is true, he will resist, might even fight back. It isn't worth the risk."

Arthur knew he was right, but was still angry at the 'following' crack, "It sounds to me like you afraid of a fat old man."

Hans knew Arthur was trying to needle him, but it didn't really matter. "With Garneau there, it means that Claude will be too, plus his 'French Maid', and the others. Before, it would just be the old cook and maids, far less chance of someone being a hero. There are too many people for one person."

"You are right, of course, so what are you thinking?"

"It occurred to me that we could take both the Falcon's collection and Dr. Schaeffer's as well. As a bonus, we grab the Eye of God, and call it our retirement savings."

Arthur liked this idea very much, but was distracted. "Are they being followed?"

"Of course, that is what we are doing…what are you talking about?"

"The car that pulled out before us is still on their tail, after three turns."

Hans looked more closely, but wasn't sure. They sat in silence, until the traffic slowed to a crawl on Broadway. "You seen that yet?" Arthur asked, pointing at a marquee.

"What?"

"The Pajama Game. Garneau made me go to it with him earlier in the year."

"I read it got great reviews, but no, I haven't seen it."

"I didn't realize it at the time, but I had read Bissell's novel, Seven and a Half Cents. I didn't know they had turned it into a musical, until I was reading the program."

"Are they turning?" Hans said.

"I don't know if they will tour, but I would think they might."

Hans pointing ahead, "No, the Falcon and Patrick, are they TURNING."

"Sorry, And yes."

They turned too, as did the car which was following Patrick's car.

* * *

Arthur and Hans had fallen behind, when they found the car, and Randy, the Studebaker was gone.

Chapter Fifty-Five

Patrick and Katarina looked at each other. He had a blank expression on his face; she had a glimmer of hope in her eyes. It was obvious she had an idea. Patrick hadn't faced tough situations before; his planning had always kept him at arm's length. He thought about how he wished he could just give them the Eye of God and walk away, but that wasn't an option.

Katarina felt a little bit better, seeing that Patrick wasn't scared, but she could tell he was at a loss. The situation looked bleak, but she had one skill, better than the rest. She could weave a story. If she did it well, she might be able to keep them alive long enough to escape. She knew the history of the artifact and she knew that they couldn't kill them until it was found. She hoped they spoke English well enough to understand her, as a good story not understood, isn't very helpful.

The thought crossed her mind that maybe Arthur and Hans had been able to keep up. That gave her hope. Had they even noticed the other car following her? It was a fifty/fifty proposition, at best. What she needed was to bring in Henry. *He's smart, but can I get him a message? And what should that message be?*

The car slowed to a stop and the driver got out at a pay phone. The man in the passenger seat said something to them in Greek.

The tone was not threatening, it was calm, but the smile afterwords was unnerving. The driver got back in and they started off again.

Katrina looked back and there wasn't anyone behind them, so it seemed that Arthur and Hans had not kept up. The car turned twice and then pulled into a deserted parking lot. There were two more cars and a truck. There must have been eight guys standing around, but she couldn't tell if there were more in the cars. They were taken out of the cars at gun point and forced into the back of the truck. The sound of a lock told them that their captors weren't taking any chances of them jumping out of the back.

This was a break. Katarina could talk to Patrick and get on the same page.

* * *

Henry's mood had been dampened by the news that Katarina was involved. Mike hadn't mentioned that she was the Falcon. Henry didn't see any point in denying it and told them Katarina's history and her knowledge of art. He wasn't sure when she had gotten involved in the world of stolen art, but it seemed obvious to him that she was the Falcon.

"Maybe she just works for the Falcon?" Celine offered, feeling Henry's pain.

"It's possible, but my gut tells me otherwise."

Professor Brookert, "So where are we at? It seems like we have fulfilled our contract with Dr. Schaeffer, but we still don't know who killed Mickey."

Mike, "We also know of a crime about to be committed, namely selling stolen merchandise. It's likely there are three other murders which were part of this deal. Maybe we should call the chief and put an end to this, let them sort it out downtown."

"You might be right, Mike. I want to catch the bastard who killed Mike, but waiting until I have proof, might be a mistake. He's dead. I've accepted it and all that's left is to lock up the killer. There's only one concern and that is Dr. Schaeffer, I don't feel right about letting him get caught, even if he is guilty of buying stolen art. Are you okay with that, Mike?"

Mike wasn't okay with it, but he understood Henry, and his loyalty to his friends. It didn't surprise Mike that Henry would be as loyal to his clients, too. He had learned that from Mickey. "No, I understand."

It was decided they would all be in the office by 7:00 a.m. Henry needed to sleep on his plan.

* * *

Patrick looked at her, "You have an idea. I can see it."

"We have been doing business a long time, my friend. I'm not going to sugar coat it; I think our chances are not very good. Once they realize we don't know where it is, they won't have any reason not to put us both down."

"You make us sound like dogs."

"To them, we are lower than dogs. You have their 'Eye' and they want it back."

"I'm starting to rethink my decision to handle this piece." Patrick was nervous, losing his game face, and turned to humor, feebly.

Katarina's mind, working like a world class chess player, "As long as we offer the hope of recovery, they'll not risk losing the 'Eye', by killing us. If they believe there is a chance of delivering the 'Eye', it will keep us alive. It's not a priceless artifact to them; it is the center of their way of life. They've been searching for it for years. This may be the closest they've come to getting it back."

Patrick felt inadequate for asking, "What is this thing? I thought it was just a really old, and priceless, watch."

"If we live, I'll tell you all about it. I'll need you to follow my lead."

Patrick nodded and she leaned back, closing her eyes. He considered himself a master tactician, but couldn't imagine how she planned to deliver it. If they lived, he wouldn't wait around for the story, he was retired from the stolen art business.

* * *

Henry drove past his apartment, but decided to go to his house instead. Her smell would still be on his pillow, and that would just cloud his mind. He crossed the bridge and was home before he knew it. His brain was on autopilot. Henry knew he would need to confront her, he knew she had either killed Mickey or knew who did. He wasn't sure which was worse, the thought of her sharing his bed, after having killed his mentor, or her going to the wake knowing who had.

She wasn't the smart, funny, beautiful woman he knew from before, she was just a woman. He tried to figure a reason he could accept, but he knew why, greed. The conversation he would have with her, started to play in his mind. Henry grabbed a beer and sat down at his kitchen table. Henry could hear her excuses, her justifications, her blaming someone else, or her admitting it and begging for mercy. None of the stories had a happy ending.

Henry thought about what Mike had said and though he wanted to feel sorry for himself, he knew he couldn't. Tomorrow, they would let the captain know everything. Henry needed to figure out how to bring down Patrick, stop the auction, keep Dr. Schaeffer out of it, and get Katarina to confess or give up the person who killed Mike. There were enough cops who loved Mickey that simply storming the auction would net everyone involved. He was sure that could be arranged. But how could he keep his client out of the fray? In fact, he needed Dr. Schaeffer to let him in on the location of the auction.

There was one thing which bothered him, still. It wasn't just Mickey's murder, someone had murdered the two Greek guys, and Mr. Brown in his brown suit. He got out his notebook and flipped through the pages. He found the page, Mr. Brown beaten to death in his home. He just couldn't imagine Katarina beating someone to death. Obviously, it was someone from her organization. Henry didn't have proof that she was the Falcon, just his gut telling him it was her. It was his same gut which said she didn't kill Mr. Brown and those two drunken Greeks. Katarina must have a team.

That made sense, he thought. If she was this legendary collector, who had remained anonymous, she would have needed help. She would have needed people to deliver messages, to watch her back, and to make payments. Henry didn't know what it took to be a world class stolen art collector, but he was sure it wasn't a one woman job.

For a moment there was slightest glimmer of hope. Maybe a lieutenant had knocked off Mickey? He started to rerun the imaginary conversation again, this time, with a plausible explanation. She didn't order the hit, it was his decision, and she didn't approve. He would ask her why she didn't tell him the truth. The glimmer of hope died, when he realized that there still wasn't an answer he could accept.

Henry went to bed and slept for almost two hours, until a loud bang, from his basement, woke him up.

Chapter Fifty-Six

Henry was startled and couldn't imagine what had just exploded. He grabbed the baseball bat in the corner and made his way through his house, turning on one light at a time. On the basement stairs, with his mind a bit clearer, realized it must be the closet. There wasn't anyone downstairs so he opened the door and lying on the floor was a New York Times.

The date October 16, 1988; thirty-three and one half years from where Henry stood, and he knew it must have a clue. His closet, with its gift from the future, seemed to give him the little extra nudge in the right direction, whenever he needed it. Henry had suspected that the newspapers left this week had been put there from the near future, but he had found them too late. He had been bothered by this, blaming himself for missing a chance to save Mickey.

Henry took the paper upstairs, dropped it on the table, and started a pot of coffee. He had spent enough hours thinking about the how and why of his closet, without coming up with any ideas, that he took it all in stride. He looked at the front page and read a few articles. This was almost as cool as the machine which played movies in color. Reading about the future was exciting, but he couldn't indulge his desire to think about all the strange things advertised and written about. This paper contains a clue, something which will point him in the right direction and help with the next move.

Henry didn't expect a huge headline from 1988, screaming 'Henry Wood Saves Day' with an article describing what he had done in 1955. It would be subtle. He read a few more articles and nothing. The coffee was finished brewing, so he poured himself a cup, added sugar and cream and sat back down. Out of habit he pulled out the sports section. What he saw next shook him to the core.

He just stared at it. The headline almost stopped his heart. It wasn't the clue, it was something much worse. Everything he should be thinking about seemed to be nothing but a din of background noise. He read the article, twice, and just didn't understand. It appears that the night before, in front of 55,983 people, in California, the Los Angeles Dodgers won the first game of the World Series against somebody called the Oakland Athletics, 5-4. His love of baseball and the Dodgers made this the most horrible revelation he could imagine. *How could they leave?*

The coffee was good. Henry had a hard time getting back to the paper, he wondered if he would live long enough to find out who wins game two and the series. If he did make it to October 1988, he would have to remember to put a few bucks on game one. That made him smile, but only a little. The worst part was living with the specter of their move hanging over his head. He would go to more games this year, just in case. He assumed it didn't happen for at least 20 or 30 years though, they were just too loved right now, to leave anytime soon. The cup was empty, but he wasn't up in the middle of the night, to think about baseball. He needed a second cup.

After another 20 minutes of reading he came to an article about the tearing down of a building in the Bowery. This was it. He didn't know the relevance, but the description in the article sounded like it was one of Randy's hiding places. The article talked about how the clever hiding place looked like it had been created and then gone unnoticed by every tenant since. If they hadn't been tearing down walls, it might have never been discovered.

Henry decided he was up now. He got in the shower to get ready for the day.

At his apartment in the city, his phone rang again. It was the third call he had missed.

Chapter Fifty-Seven

It was not what Katarina expected. They sat in leather chairs in a large space. In front of them was a table, with a pitcher of water, and a couple of glasses. On the other side of the table sat a gentleman with a white beard, drinking a glass of wine. The floor was concrete, but had a nice Oriental rug on it. There were very bright lights surrounding them. The lights were to overpowering to see the walls. Katarina sensed there were people, beyond the lights, but couldn't tell how many.

The strangest part was that Katerina couldn't remember being moved from the truck to the chairs. But here they were, the show was about to begin.

"My name is…not important…nor is yours to me. I have only one concern and that is to recover what is rightfully the property of our little organization and right this wrong."

Katarina wanted to establish some credibility with their captors. She had an idea how she might pull it off, but feared it might blow up in her face. She went for it. She leaned forward and calmly poured a glass of water and then said, "You must be Thorstians."

The man showed the slightest hint of being impressed. "We are. There are few who have ever heard of us. We like our privacy."

His tone made her think she might have misplayed the hand, but folding wasn't an option, so she continued, "I've been searching for the Eye of God for a long time. I didn't have anything to do with stealing it from you, but I do admit to being interested in buying it. I should mention, my friend here didn't steal it either. He is merely the broker."

"Is that true?"

Patrick nodded. He was at a loss for something helpful to say.

"I see you are a man of few words. To be truthful, we know you didn't steal it, we know exactly what you are…a fence."

He found his voice. "Begging your pardon, but I am not 'A Fence', I am 'The Fence'." Proverbs 16:18 suddenly came to mind, 'Pride goeth before destruction, and a haughty spirit before a fall', and Patrick realized that he should be a little more modest. He wasn't sure if he would get too many more chances, though.

The man across them seemed neither amused nor offended. "I really don't care if you are the greatest fence to have ever lived. We have this situation today, because you are trying to sell something which is not yours, or your clients. Which brings us to my two concerns, who is your client, and where is our box?"

Patrick and Katarina had agreed to be honest about how the box was temporarily misplaced, because of the untimely death of Randy. Patrick went into great detail about his arrangement with Randy, explaining why he trusted him, and the advantages to hiding valuable works of art this way. He wanted to make sure that their captors understood that he was not making up a story and to do that, he needed to explain his reasoning. If he had simply said, "I don't have it, it is hidden, and I don't know where it is." They wouldn't have believed him, or worse, they would have tried to beat it out of him.

The old Greek man listened. When the story was done he sat quietly for a moment. "I am not a violent man. I just wish to have returned what rightfully belongs to me and my associates. But you can see where we have a problem. Though your story seems quite convincing, it doesn't help me achieve my goals. Let us start with something you can tell me. Who is your client?"

Patrick didn't like the idea of telling him, but the situation was looking rather bleak. "To be honest, I am not sure I could pronounce it, but if you give me a pencil, I will write it down for you."

A large man appeared from out of the darkness with a piece of paper and a pencil. He had a machine gun looped around his neck and looked like he might enjoy getting to use it. Patrick wrote down the name and slid it across the table to their host. The man with the beard read the name. He did not look happy.

The sound of anxious footsteps was all that could be heard. Someone whispered in Greek. Katarina guessed it was Greek for, "Who is it?" The man in the chair said something back in a harsh tone. The walking around ceased and there was silence.

Katarina sensing her moment said, "I believe I have an idea, which will help you locate 'The Eye', but I have a condition."

She was wrong about it being her moment. He exploded, "A condition!" He stood up and disappeared from the light, returning with a pistol. He pointed it at her, then waved the gun to his left and fired. Patrick's hand went to the right side of his head and cupped his bleeding ear. "You are not in a position to be making demands!" He then disappeared from the lit area again, and they could hear his heavy footsteps behind them.

Katarina looked over at Patrick. His expression was a mixture of shock and horror. The blood was trickling between his fingers. She felt a hand come over top of the leather chair and pull her chin upward. All she could see was the barrel of the gun pressed between her eyes and a giant meaty hand holding the trigger.

"Where is it?" he said, in a voice of tempered rage.

"I don't know. But I believe my idea is the only way you'll find it. I still have one condition."

The man in the beard's hand began to shake and the

accompanying silence was the scariest thing anyone in the room had ever not heard. The sound of the hammer being lowered eased the tension ever so slightly. The man's voice, having returned to a calm state, said something in his native tongue. A few men came forward and grabbed Patrick and took him away.

He sat back down. "Everyone, leave!"

The room was emptied and the sound of a heavy metal door closing, was followed by quiet. Katarina, with the nerves of a fighter ace, stared into the man's eyes. "I know a man who knows where the first hiding place was and I believe he may have some ideas about where it is now."

"And you will tell me who this man is, if I agree to your…'One Condition'…what is that condition?"

"I want to ask the 'Eye' one question.'

This made the man smile. She was a true believer. He leaned back in his chair and folded his hands together under his chin. "So that is your condition. Nothing about letting the two of you go?"

"I believed you when you said you were not a violent man."

"Do you still believe that?" He said, looking at the chair where Patrick had been sitting.

"I do. You have been searching for 'The Eye' for many years. Once you have it, I don't see any reason for you to kill us, as you haven't committed a crime."

"And what of kidnapping?"

She smiled, "Let's just say that I have done some things, in my past, which make 'going to the police', a bad idea. And you know of Patrick's line of work. I think I can speak for both of us, when I say, we won't be pressing charges."

This seemed to satisfy the man. "I agree. What is his name?"

"While I believe you are not a violent man, I am not willing to put him at risk. Get me a phone and I'll call him and set it all up. He should be able to find it in a day or two."

The man stood up and nodded. He walked out of the room. She

sat there alone until Patrick returned. They had bandaged up his ear and he sat back down. "I assume he liked your idea. And what is your condition?"

"It is personal."

"It got me shot!"

"I don't care."

Chapter Fifty-Eight

At 4:00 a.m., in the city that never sleeps, one wouldn't notice much difference between the hour before or the one after. Henry noticed Bobby's office light was on. This almost struck him as strange, were it not for 'strange' being Bobby's normal. He knocked. From what seemed like a long ways away, tiny feet could be heard scampering towards the door.

Bobby didn't show any surprise at seeing Henry. "Hello Henry, come to answer your phone, have you?"

"My phone?"

"Yes, it started ringing a few hours ago, and has gone off every thirty minutes since."

"I wonder who could be calling?" He said, though he was sure he knew.

Bobby looked at his watch, "We best stop talking as it is about to ring..."

It was easy to hear in the quiet office hall, and Henry walked briskly to the door. He had to pick the lock, as he hadn't gotten a key from Celine, yet. He grabbed the phone on Celine's desk.

"Hey"

"Its Katarina."

"I haven't seen you all day. I thought you might call and make me take you to dinner or something."

"I would love a bit of 'or something', but I am in trouble."

Henry sat down in Celine's chair and leaned back. It seemed like the misery of the last week, was behind him, and he had his mind back. He let her comment hang there for a moment and then said, "I figured as much. Hot art can burn one's fingers."

"I need your help finding something. It's life and death."

"That is a little bit cliché, don't you think?"

A man's voice came on the phone. "Do you know where the Eye of God is hidden?"

"I like direct, but only when I know who is asking the question."

"I am a determined man, who only wants what is rightfully his."

"We all have wants."

The Greek man was intrigued by the comment. "And what are your wants? Mr...."

Henry had noticed that Katarina hadn't used his name. Every other time they had spoken on the phone she always said 'Henry' in a certain way. This time though, straight to the point. He decided there might be a reason. "I want answers to a few questions, that is all."

"You may ask me anything you like about the Eye of God, if it induces you to return it to me."

"Let's be clear. I don't have it, but I know where it may be found. As for my questions, it is the woman who called that has the answers."

The Greek man looked at Katarina, not sure where this was going, "You don't want money?"

"No. I want her to answer my questions, but I'll need your help."

"I am listening."

Henry talked and the Greek man said nothing. The call ended with the Greek man slamming the phone down just as Henry had instructed.

Chapter Fifty-Nine

Arthur and Hans had spent the entire night looking for the Falcon. All they had to go on, was the make and model of car which had been in front of them. They assumed that the people who shot the driver had left with the Falcon and Patrick. At around 5:00 a.m., they gave up and stopped to eat at a diner.

There were quite a few people getting their day started, so they spoke in hushed tones. Hans ate a slice of toast while shaking his head, "I don't know."

"Who were those guys?" Arthur asked while stirring his coffee.

"I couldn't even hazard a guess. I know this, if someone has taken Patrick, then they are after 'The Eye'. So, I think we can assume the auction won't take place today and likely won't happen at all."

"What I want to know is how they found him?"

"No idea."

"Could it have been one of the other collectors?"

"No, they are all gutless old men. This was too clean a snatch and grab; it was professional." Hans almost sounded impressed.

"It beats me. I wonder…"

Hans looked up while eating his eggs.

"You think it might have been the guys it was taken from?"

Hans thought about this, "That may be a good guess. So we are looking for some Greeks."

Arthur shrugged, "But does it matter?"

"It may not. Our plan is pretty well shot."

"It seems our window of opportunity has closed. I dread the thought of going back to Andre, even if he is 'new and improved'."

Hans nodded, "I know how you feel, my friend. To get so close to finally being free of Dr. Schaeffer, and now, we won't even have our cut from the Falcon."

"Huh, hadn't thought about that, but you're right. The extra money was nice."

They sat lamenting their lost lives of leisure, which had been driving them for so long. The other patrons continued to come and go, but they stayed, drinking coffee and feeling sorry for themselves. The waitress was starting to give them dirty looks, but they ignored her. Hans, not one to give up, finally had had enough.

"Let's be logical." Hans said leaning back and changing his tone.

"Let's. What are you thinking?"

"If we find the Falcon, we are fine. We have lost some time, but there will be other auctions. You could work your way into the house of another collector and leave Garneau behind."

Arthur liked the sound, "True."

"We get back in the game, set up our original plan with Dr. Schaeffer and someone else, and make our big score."

Hans had a way of finding clarity in a heavy fog of despair. Arthur felt better, "You are right, we have lost only time and effort. Nobody knows who the Falcon is, or that we work with her. She will continue to collect and pay us for our information and help. It will be easier than when we started, because you are already trusted by Dr. Schaeffer."

"Speaking of which, I am expected at his place. His nerves will be on edge, not knowing when the auction is to take place. If any of Patrick's minions shows up with word, I'll be there to get the latest. I can make some calls, looking for the Greeks."

"That sounds like a plan. I better be off to see what the new and improved, though still disgusting, Andre has in store for me today. It will likely involve orphans and puppies, unless I miss my guess. I'll try not to kill him or myself. If you hear anything, call me, I'll make an excuse to get away. We aren't beat yet, my friend."

They paid and walked out. Waiting to cross the street, Hans had an idea. It was a long shot but it was low risk and he was sure he could make Dr. Schaeffer think it was his idea. The game wasn't over; it was just the start of the fourth quarter.

Chapter Sixty

She could now see the faintest outline of light around the blacked out windows. Katarina sat in her chair, feet up on the table, with a blanket, staring at a small pin light coming through one of the panes. She had watched it change from black to a faint glow and now a stream of orange light. Sleep had been impossible to come by, so she just thought.

She thought about her life and her quest some, but mostly she thought about Henry. She remembered how he was when they met. Always the gentleman, opening doors, paying for dinner, and letting her choose which movie. He never made a pass or gave any indication how he might feel, but on occasion, she would catch how he looked at her, usually in a reflection. She knew and played dumb, and now, these many years later, after a couple nights in his bed, wondered why.

Katarina was worried. The call hadn't gone like she planned. He seemed to really know where it was, but his voice was cold. Faced with the real possibility that her final moments may be spent sitting in this chair, she considered her stained soul, and the truth of who she had become was unavoidable. She had used Henry, because she could. It was this way with all the men from her past, but they deserved it, they had souls blacker than hers, they had their agendas and she used that against them. Revenge is a sweet dish, best served cold they say. She thought of how she had used Henry's affection for her, to blind him to the truth. It had worked to keep him in the dark. The taste of the truth was foul.

The reaction from her Greek captor, so completely caught her off guard that she almost tried to run. Her instincts had told her it would be fatal, and she listened. Still it was a mystery what they had said, and since he stormed out of the room, she had not heard a word.

Patrick stretched, waking from a fitful sleep, "It must be morning. I wonder if it will be our last?" He said with a smile, which seemed oddly optimistic, considering.

"I fear it might be."

"Now don't be that way, love, I'm sure that a clever lad like Henry will ride to our rescue on his mighty steed. Or maybe he won't, who knows? But I could really use a cup of coffee."

She looked at him. It seemed that all traces of Father Patrick were gone. She wondered if this were the real man behind the collar.

"It may be my last day, but it is my first day without that choker around my neck, and I feel great."

"Slept well did you?"

"Not well, but I slept. I had a dream of a lassie back in Dublin. I haven't seen her since I was a wee one." His voice had changed and now his accent was coming through. "She had raven black hair and a serious look that could put the fear of the Almighty in one's heart. If you had the stones to get past the serious though, you were in for a treat. It was good to see her again."

Katarina wanted to be disgusted with his flippant attitude, but he was too damn charming, and the worst part was she knew he wasn't even trying.

They heard the heavy door open and two large men brought in plates with some donuts and a couple of cups of coffee. They said it was from their boss, apologized for the meager fair, and then left. They didn't' sound sincere, they sounded annoyed.

"I think the help is getting antsy," Katarina observed.

Patrick grabbed a donut.

"I have been trying to figure out what made our host so mad."

"Perhaps your boy Henry told him to piss off, he was keeping 'The Eye' for himself."

She hadn't considered this angle. It hurt her pride and now she was mad. "You don't know him, he isn't like us, and he wouldn't keep it knowing it would…"

"What?…get us killed? Sure he would, everyone has a price. His just happens to be north of 5 million somewhere, I would guess. So how much were you willing to bid?"

"Why don't you shut up?" She had had enough of Patrick. His laughter at her anger just made her more furious.

Patrick took another donut.

Katarina sat in silence, ignoring the occasional comments from the other chair. She went back to thinking about Henry. She went back to when they met. It helped her feel a little better and made her feel much worse.

When the heavy footsteps of their Greek host stormed into the room, they both sat up straight. He picked up the phone from the table by his chair and slammed the phone down in front of Katarina, and said, "Tell your friend I will pay him the money!" He then started muttering something loudly in Greek and left the room. The two men who brought the donuts came in and grabbed Patrick and dragged him out of the room, spilling his coffee.

She stared at the phone almost afraid to dial.

Chapter Sixty-One

The phone rang and Henry answered. He was expecting the call, but not this call. He recognized Han's voice.

"Mr. Wood, I wasn't sure when you would be in the office today."

"Hello, Hans."

"Dr. Schaeffer was pleased with how it went yesterday."

"I thought it went well, too."

"There is a problem though."

Henry was not sure where this was going and didn't want to stay on the line too long. He looked at his watch, 7:01.

"Yes?"

"I would like to see you in person, if you wouldn't mind."

"I am actually pretty busy this morning…"

"It's urgent."

Henry considered saying no, but his gut told him it might be worth hearing him out.

"How long will it take you to get here?"

"Not long."

"I'll put on the coffee."

* * *

The Greek man yelled, "Well?"

Katarina didn't like the sound of her answer in her head, but it was true. "It was busy."

"Try again!"

She dialed the number. It rang, once, then twice. Henry's voice lacked warmth. "Hey…"

"Do you have an answer for me?"

She whispered, almost saying his name, "Hen…" She took a breath, "What is going on?" Fatigue and fear had stripped away her ability to control herself. She was scared, it came through in her voice, and she hated the weak sound of it, but there wasn't anything she could do.

Slowly and measured he said, "Did the Greek man give an answer?"

"He said he will pay you the money." She sounded small and defeated.

"Call me back in one hour. Tell him we have a deal."

"Henry…", she said, sounding desperate, "I am in serious trouble here, what is…" The phone clicked off.

The Greek man came back into the room and put the phone on the table next to his chair. He was suddenly calm and smoking a cigarette. It smelled awful.

"They are Turkish. My wife hates the smell too. A filthy habit, I admit, but I like them. It appears we have reached a deal with your friend. I have to admit, he is a cool customer. He played his hand well. We have reached a deal and the thought of putting this whole mess behind us, has improved my mood considerably." He looked past her, took a long pull from his cigarette and made a motion with his hand.

From the other room, the muffled but distinct sounds of a pistol could be heard. She heard the body fall, and then the heavy door closed. The Greek man's smile was slight and terrifying. "Yes, soon it will all be over."

She started to talk, but nothing came out. She tried again, her voice trembling, "What deal? We had a deal too."

"Yes, I have some vague recollection of something, but my mind isn't what it used to be. I don't recall the deal you made including a payout to your friend. It seems that this new deal trumps the old one. I would say I am sorry, but you disgust me."

"I thought you were a man of your word."

"I was under the impression you were better at reading people." He stood up, with a smile, enjoying the little joke he'd made.

She leapt from her chair, fear and adrenaline taking over. She swung wildly and he grabbed her wrist. The second blow was equally ineffective. "I would kill you now, but you are the only one who knows his number. So it has bought you an hour."

He flung her back in the chair and walked out.

Chapter Sixty-Two

Hans knocked lightly and opened the door. Henry, in the back, told him to come in. Hans hung his hat and coat on the hall tree, walked into Henry's office, closing the door behind him. Henry started to get up, but Hans waved it off.

"No need to stand Mr. Woods. I will be brief."

Henry sat back down, motioning to the chair. "How may I help?"

"I wasn't entirely truthful with you on the phone, as Dr. Schaeffer was in the room. Though it is true, he is concerned about the auction, as he hasn't heard from Patrick, that's not why I am here."

"Oh?"

"You see Mr. Wood, I serve two masters." Hans paused and took a breath. "I assist Dr. Schaeffer, but I also work for the 'Falcon'. In fact, I only work for the doctor, to keep an eye on him."

"An art spy, as it were."

"Yes. Myself and Andre Garneau's man Arthur, were planted by the Falcon years ago. It is our job to keep her, er, the Falcon, informed about their financial means, which items they truly want, and then to, when it serves her needs, help one or the other win a bid, or lose entirely."

"Art collecting is a dirty business. So what is it you want, though I am not saying I'll help. Frankly speaking, I find your little revelation to be revolting. Dr. Schaeffer seems like a good man."

Hans had to bite his tongue, his hatred of Dr. Schaeffer was about to boil over. "Yes, but business is business, as they say. The Falcon has been kidnapped, along with Father Patrick. We need you to find out where they are, so we might get them out."

Henry leaned back in his chair and looked at Hans. They both knew it was Henry's turn to talk and he just let the silence hang there, choking Hans. Henry could see that under his calm blank expression, was a look of desperation. "What makes you think I can find them?"

"You have connections, specifically within the police department. They were taken last night, from a car, and the driver was killed. You are a very bright detective, and I was impressed with how much you learned for Dr. Schaeffer, so I am confident you will dig up something."

Henry was confident that the flattery did not impress him at all. "It will cost you."

"How much?"

"$10,000…each."

"That seems awfully steep."

"I have standards about the type of client I will take, and frankly, knowing you now, you fall short. Oh and did I mention it needs to be cash…upfront."

Hans walked out to his coat and returned with the money, dropping on the desk. "Okay, here is your money, now…"

"Now nothing, I won't have you dictating terms. You and Arthur be ready, when I find out their location, and I will. I'll call you. You may think I am some small time private dick, but I care about Katarina, as much as you do…maybe more."

Hans knew he had been played. Henry was already working to save the Falcon, but finding that out, just cost him and Arthur

$20,000. Hans wrote a phone number down and dropped it on the desk. He didn't say goodbye.

Henry got up and put the money in the safe. He called Mike, but didn't get an answer. He was probably on his way, as was everyone else. He wouldn't have much time to get the pieces in place. And there was the one wild card; could he trust the Greek man? If he couldn't, well it wouldn't just be Katarina in a tight spot.

Henry thought about Mickey, he thought about the $20,000 and smiled. Mickey would have approved. He thought about some of the tight spots they had been in, and the thrill of getting out. The best part was always the drinks after, listening to Mickey tell the story. Listening to the embellishments was always entertaining.

Henry flipped open his notebook and went to the two pages he hadn't decoded. He gave it one look and pulled out his pencil. Two minutes later he had it all worked out. He had everything he needed right in front of him, courtesy of Michael Thomas Moore.

Chapter Sixty-Three

The phone rang, and Henry picked it up without speaking.

"I waited the hour. What do we do now?" Katrina said, sounding shaky.

Henry took a bit of the edge off of his voice, "We are going to get you out of there, but it is going to require a bit of finesse. You're going to have to trust me."

"I do."

"Will you do what I tell you, when the time comes? Our lives may depend upon it."

"Yes, whatever you need me to do."

"Put the Greek man on the phone."

A few seconds later the voice changed. "Hello, Sir. I've followed your instructions, now let's discuss the exchange."

Henry said, "You did a good job, she sounds petrified. I'm ready to take you to the 'Eye'. Leave a couple of your men to watch her. It is in a building not far from there, and the neighborhood should be pretty quiet at that hour."

The Greek man had walked out of the room. Henry gave him all the details, and the time they would meet.

* * *

Celine said, "It sounds dangerous to me."

Professor Brookert said, "I agree with Celine, but I also don't see any other way."

Hans and Arthur stood by the desk, behind them Mike, all with concerned looks on their faces. "They will be expecting a double cross, so that is why we have to keep everything in balance. That is why we are meeting at 10:00 p.m., because everything has to be perfect. There can't be any reason for him to change his mind. If he gets what he wants, he will disappear into the night, and we will get Katarina and Patrick back."

Arthur said, "It still seems like they have the edge."

"Look, You, Hans, the Professor and I will take my car. The Greek man will follow with most of his men. We will take them to the building with the 'Eye' hidden in it. The Greek man will give me the address where they are holding our friends. Then the three of you will stay with them, while I drive to wherever they are keeping Katarina and Patrick. When I get there, I'll give the phone number to their two guys, who will call their boss. It's to a pay phone outside the building. Once he gets on the phone, then they let me into the room to check on Katarina. At this point, I tell them where to find the 'Eye'. It will take a little while to break through the wall, since I don't know how to open the trap door. Once they have the 'Eye', have checked it out and are satisfied, then he will call back. I have looked into it, and there is a phone in the room, where it is hidden. He calls back, tells his guys he has got it, and they leave. Then I call back, to the pay phone, where the professor is waiting, and give the all clear. At that point, Arthur and Hans you two leave the front of the building with the professor and they see you drive off."

Arthur said, "I don't understand why he won't just tell his guys to shoot you and Katarina."

"You and Hans will be covering their only exit. They may have you outnumbered, but if they want to sneak quietly out of the building and get away with their artifact, they can't risk a noisy shootout. He is a smart man and knows it is best we just go our separate ways."

Professor Brookert said, "Do I get a gun?"

"You ever fired a gun?"

"No, but I know which end the bullet comes out of."

"In that case…no."

Mike said, "I am not clear on my role."

"You will already be at the building with the 'Eye'. You follow me to where they have Katarina and Patrick. You are my back-up. Keep out of site, they don't need to know I have an insurance policy."

Celine was making another pot of coffee, her face showed concern. "It just seems like there are too many moving parts, too many cogs which could break, and cause your perfect little plan to go horribly wrong."

"I appreciate your vote of confidence."

There were some light chuckles.

She wasn't convinced and said, "I am not ready to start looking for another job. If you do get killed, I am taking the petty cash."

Henry said, "Okay, everyone back here at nine."

With that, everyone headed out, except Mike. Celine started to clean up the coffee cups, while Mike and Henry went over it one more time.

When they reached the street Hans whispered to Arthur, "I have a new plan. We may make those early retirements after all."

Chapter Sixty-Four

Hans and Arthur got out onto the street and walked a ways without talking. The morning air was still and the exhaust from the traffic seemed thicker than usual. A taxi splashed a puddle at them, as Arthur lit a cigarette and then motioned towards a restaurant across the street.

Inside it was dark. The lunch crowd hadn't arrived yet. In fact, they were the only ones there. They could hear the kitchen staff prepping for the day, pots and pans being shuffled about. Hans requested a booth in the back. The waiter took their order and hurried off. Both men were thinking about their next move, or more accurately, Hans was thinking, while Arthur was trying to guess what he might have in mind. The food arrived and Hans started to lay out his plan.

"If we had the 'Eye', I could set up a meeting between you and Dr. Schaeffer. You two have never met, correct?"

"It is strange, for as much as I know about him, no we have never met. But I guess that was by design. I may not like the Falcon, but I give her credit for her planning. Yes, I could pose as the original seller, explaining that I was able to recover it, when everything went south."

"We can figure out the cover story later. Right now I have only one question, can we take it from the Greek man and his men. It could get a little bit messy."

"Yes, you are right, but you know I am not afraid to get my hands dirty. They will be on guard though, so we are going to need some help. There won't be an element of surprise."

Hans cuts his steak as he thinks about how they might pull it off. Arthur starts to name off some guys who they could employ, though he knows Hans is only barely listening. The waiter refills their water glasses, and then takes away the salads. When he is out of ear shot, Hans continues, "I think we will need four extra guys."

"We don't know how many men they will have?"

"Yes, we may be out numbered, but we may still be able to get the jump on them."

"How is that?"

"When Henry gives the all clear, we drive away, as planned. We pull around the corner, pop the professor, then park and head back into the building. They will be worrying about loading the 'Eye' up and at least two men will be required to move it. If we use silencers, we may be able to take out a few of them, before they even know what has hit them."

"You think we should kill the professor? If we do, Henry will know it was us. It's Henry's car, so we let the professor drive, then after we are out of sight, ask him to let us out."

Hans smiled, "That is why we make a good team; you see the simple elegant solution, when I do not."

"Thank you."

Hans continues, "So we make our way back to the Greeks, take the 'Eye', and set up the sale with Dr. Schaeffer."

"If we move quickly, we can blow town tomorrow, as wealthy men."

"We may not get to settle our scores with Schaeffer and Garneau, but I am tired, and ready to put this all behind us."

Arthur nodded his head. "Yes my friend, I am tired too. A simple life, some wine, maybe a woman, and my greatest worry, is when to roll out of bed in the morning. There is one problem though."

"Yes, the Falcon. She won't be happy, us pulling the double cross, cutting her out, selling it to Dr. Schaeffer."

"She has contacts all over the world, some pretty dangerous people, too. I couldn't even guess how much money she has squirreled away in Swiss accounts. She will come after us. It will hardly be a life of leisure, if we have to look over our shoulders constantly."

Hans finishes his steak, while considering Arthur's last point. "We had planned on killing her originally, so I guess we take care of her, before we leave town. After we get the 'Eye', we head back to Henry's office. They should all be there."

"Yes, but we can't kill them all. There will already be plenty of Greek bodies lying around; add an office full to the equation and it would be too much. Also won't it look suspicious, us being left off by the professor, then showing up again?"

"Great points, our plan seems to be flawed. Or more precisely, my plan is flawed. Your ideas have been right on the mark."

"How about we grab the 'Eye', and then tomorrow, we present it to the Falcon."

Hans is intrigued. "Go on…"

"She will be ecstatic and pay us well. Unlike the paintings and sculptures, she won't be able to move it alone. The Falcon will need at least one of us to help her. We finally get taken to her stash."

"Oh you are brilliant."

"Thank you. I'm sure you have figured out the rest…"

"We wait to kill her and get our bonuses, the 'Eye', and her sizable collection."

"Yes, but the best part, we leave her body in her secret stash, which will keep anyone from finding it for a long time. Then we sell the 'Eye' to Dr. Schaeffer, and leave town as planned."

"Okay, we need to round up our helpers."

With that they paid their bill and left.

Chapter Sixty-Five

Henry drove, professor Brookert sat in the passenger seat and Arthur and Hans were in the back. A black sedan and truck followed behind. Henry took W 14th street across town. The meat packing district was mostly quiet, save for a few drunks. When they pulled up to the building, Henry stopped the car next to a phone booth. He handed the keys to the professor and got out.

Two men got out of the sedan; the driver remained, as did one man in the back. Henry stopped and talked briefly with the large older man then pointed to the building across the street. He got in the back and the car drove away. The truck pulled around to the side of the building, while the two men went and stood by the phone booth. Professor Brookert slid over and got in the driver's seat. Nobody had much to say, so they just waited.

The sedan drove away and ten minutes later stopped. Henry was told which building and got out. Two men followed Henry into the building.

A few minutes later they were standing outside a heavy metal door. It looked like a room where kidnappers might hang out. A bunch of chairs, a table covered in debris from a day of prisoner watching, a deck of cards, and a radio, and some mostly empty shelving, made up the décor. One of the men opened the heavy door, and handed Henry the phone with the long cord.

He walked around the chairs and into the circle of light. Katarina looked a bit rough, but as soon as she saw Henry, leapt to her feet and threw her arms around him. Henry holding the phone in one hand, gave her a light hug, and then stepped back.

He whispered, "After I make this call, we won't have much time." Henry took out his notebook, flipped to the last page, and dialed the number. When the man in the phone booth answered, "I am here."

Katarina sat on the edge of the table, her hands clasped together between her knees. She looked tired and scared. "What now?"

"You listen." Henry paused, and then continued when she didn't say anything, "In five minutes I have to call him back. I have given him the building, but he doesn't know where the 'Eye' is hidden. We made a deal. I get 5 minutes with you, and then call him back, with my decision."

"What decision?"

"He is willing to trade the 'Eye for you or $250,000, and it is up to me. If you aren't straight with me, I am taking the money."

Katarina sat up straight, "Henry?! What do you mean?" Her voice sounding hurt.

"Listen Kat, you played me for the fool. I let you, because... well...I just couldn't help myself. It seemed real, or maybe I just wanted it to be."

"Henry, how can you say that? It was real...it is real." She reached for his hand.

"I need truth from you now, in these few minutes, or I am walking out of here. When they find out I was bluffing, they will take it out on you."

"You were bluffing? You don't know where the 'Eye' is?"

"No, never did, but you knew I could bluff well enough to get here. Wasn't that your plan?"

"Yes it was, but the way you said...well, you even convinced me."

"The clock is ticking kitten. Are you the Falcon?"

"Yes."

"Were you the Falcon when we met?"

"No, I was just me."

"Did you ever care for me?"

"Yes, of course I did, I mean, I do. Can't you tell?"

Her answers came quickly, no need to think, she was telling the truth. The next question caught her square in the jaw.

"Why did Mickey have to die?"

"He...I mean..."

"He was my best friend and you knew that. Was it you in the car?"

"No" A horrified look on her face, tears starting to fall.

"But it was you, you ordered it. You had to keep your secret. Who killed Mickey?"

"I...Henry...please let me explain."

Henry let her have it, both barrels, looking into her moist eyes. "We don't have time for your explanation. I need an answer. If we don't wipe the slate clean, if you don't tell me what you have done, I can't begin to forgive you." Giving her some hope, "I might as well take the money. Let the truth die with you. It will hurt, but not as much as your betrayal. I need to know who killed Mickey, the why can come later."

"Henry it is complicated..."

Slightly louder, a little colder, with an edge, "Who killed Mickey?"

The door opened. "It has been 5 minutes. You must call now."

Henry stood, looked at her, and then dialed. When he got the voice on the other end, "The 'Eye' is behind a wall, on the second floor. Go through the door you can see from the phone booth, there are stairs at the end of the hall. Once you get to the second floor, go down the hall, and take the first left. This hall goes for a ways; there are office doors on both sides. This hall connects to another hallway. Turn right and open the first door on the left. It is a large room, the back wall is brick. There is a hidden space behind the false wall. There is a release, but it is hard to explain how it works. Just use the sledge hammer near the corner. If you open it up near the corner, it will be safe; the boxes with the 'Eye' are at the other end of the space." Henry sat down, with the phone on his knee. "We talked." Then he listened for a moment.

Tears streamed down her face.

"I will take the…"

"No wait…it was Arthur."

Henry holding the phone, "But he works for you?!"

"Yes."

"You knew."

"Yes."

"You knew and didn't tell me."

Katarina was completely broken, sobbing into her hands, "You don't understand, I needed the 'Eye'…"

Henry stood up slowly, and then said, "You get that captain?" He hung up the phone and set it on the table.

The two men guarding the door came in and identified themselves as police officers. They carried cuffs and asked her to stand. "You have the right to remain…"

Henry walked towards the door.

Katarina ran up to him, grabbing his arm, confused. "What? What's going on?"

Henry waved off the two officers and grabbed her by the elbows. "You lost. You played everyone for the fool, even me. I let you. I couldn't help it. But I can't let you get away with Mickey's murder. I won't."

Screaming and crying, "But I need the 'Eye', I need to ask it something. I need to talk to God."

Henry gave the officers a nod and they pulled her arms behind her back. "You don't need a 2000 year old machine. You just talk. You find a quiet place and talk."

Henry walked out and down to the street. The professor pulled up and he climbed in. "Mike is over helping take Arthur and Hans down to the station. He said he would catch up with us later. The chief said you would need to make a statement, but it could wait until morning. Where to?"

"I need a drink."

"*The Dublin Rogue* it is."

Epilogue

Henry didn't have to pay for a drink all night. Everyone at *The Dublin Rogue* considered him a hero for finding Mickey's killer. He didn't feel heroic. He didn't feel like rehashing the whole story, so he mostly said, "Thanks and I'm just glad we got them." The professor and Mike filled in and recounted the main parts of the story, to those who were interested.

Around 1:00 am, Henry sat at his favorite table, in the back. He drank his beer and thought about Mickey. Luna came up and smiled, "May I join you?"

Henry poured her a beer, he was glad to see her. "Did Mike call you?"

"Yes, he said you got em."

"This is pretty late for you, don't you have to be at the bakery in a few hours."

"I have tomorrow off."

"Oh" He took a sip and looked at her, as she slid in next to him. She was familiar, comfortable, and kind. He needed that.

"You want to tell me about it? If you don't that is okay."

He didn't want to talk about it, to tell the story, but he wanted her to know. "How much do you know?"

"Mike told me you worked it out to get a confession, so even the chief got to be in on it. How did you do it?"

The bar noise seemed to fade away; he took her hand, and recounted the final act.

"I can tell you, because you know about the closet. I got a clue, a newspaper from the future."

"Really?" Luna whispered, "What did you find out?"

Henry skipped over the part about the Dodgers. He wasn't ready to deal with that open wound. "It was about a discovery of a strange empty hiding space, as a building was being remodeled. The details of the article were such, that I knew exactly where the 'Eye' had been. At the time, I didn't know what the clue meant, but I knew that eventually I would. A few hours later, I got a call…"

Henry went over the part about Hans and Arthur hiring him, told her how Katarina had called him and put him on the phone with the Greek man. Henry paused as the waitress stopped over and asked if he wanted another pitcher. He looked at Luna, who nodded, and ordered one.

"I am a good judge of people. I knew the Greek man was serious about getting the 'Eye' back, but I also sensed he didn't really want to harm Katarina or Patrick. It was strange how the plan just seemed to form before my eyes. I knew she was the 'Falcon', and had also, just before the call, cracked the rest of Mickey's code. He had figured out who she was and that Arthur and Hans worked for her, spying on her two chief rivals. It was easy to crack, once I realized she was the 'Falcon'." Henry sighed.

Luna leaned into him and whispered, "You are very clever."

"I should have figured it out before, but she…"

"It's okay. Go on with your story."

"Oh yes, where was I?"

"You were talking to the Greek man and the plan just came to you."

"Yes, I knew that Katarina had killed Mickey, or had one of her minions do it. Everyone else had been cleared, she was the only one left with motive. I just couldn't prove it. So the plan started to form. I explained to the Greek man, what I was doing, why I didn't care about his artifact, and that if he would help me, I would give it back to him. His immediate answer was yes, but it was his tone, which told me I could trust him. I needed a confession and I knew she was clever, very clever, much more than me, or I would have figured it out earlier. So we set up a schedule. First he was to get angry, then make it appear I wanted money. He agreed to make a show of killing the fence, Patrick."

"You had Patrick killed?"

"No, it was pretend. In fact, Patrick is fine. They kept him in another room after that and the Greek man and he started talking about art and fencing art. It turns out they knew some of the same people. Patrick is traveling back to Greece with the 'Eye' and its protectors. He even sent some men around to collect Patrick's stuff from his apartment."

"I'm glad." She filled her glass up and continued listening

"After the Patrick 'killing', I wanted her to stew for a while. We set up the meeting for ten o'clock in the meat packing district, because it would be quiet by then. I knew this would seem reasonable to Hans and Arthur and they went for it. What I didn't know is they would try to double cross me. They planned to rob the Greek guys, after they had the 'Eye'. What they didn't know is that three of the guys they called to help, were my buddies. Remember the three guys I told you about at the wake? The one's who worked for Father Patrick?"

"Yes, they had leather coats, thought they were tough, until you roughed them up." She said with a twinkle in her eye.

"Those are the guys. They called me as soon as they got their marching orders. So I called the Greek man and explained what was going on. He had been making sure Katarina didn't get any good sleep, so she was going to be tired and less likely to see my bluff. I still wanted to wait until after ten to confront her. I had to take a gamble. I told my Greek friend that I was ready to give him the 'Eye' now, if he would only bring a couple of guys, and keep it quiet. He agreed. The room where it was hidden wasn't used by anyone. We couldn't really smash down the wall, which had been my original plan, so we had to find the trigger to open the room. I have to give the magician credit, it was well hidden. It took an hour, but we found it. He and his men quietly loaded it into their truck. Nobody seemed to notice or care that a big box was being moved, as it was pretty busy on the loading dock. "

"Where did they take it?"

"I don't know and didn't ask. After it was in the truck, he shook my hand, and gave me this." Henry pulled out a ring with an insignia on it. "I'm an honorary 'Thorstian'."

Lana looked at the ring, grinned, and handed it back to Henry. "I won't tell anyone."

"He kept his end of the bargain. He showed up to the meeting, followed in the car, and went through everything we had set up. The difference was, they didn't need to mess around with getting the 'Eye', so they went out the back and slipped into the night. They didn't need the truck anymore, so they left it on the loading dock, so as not to tip off Arthur and Hans."

"So how did you get all the cops to show up so quickly? Mike said it was an impressive arrest."

"Between the time we found the 'Eye' and the ten o'clock meeting, I brought the chief up to speed. Mike and I went to his office and I told him the entire plan. He had about a dozen men in the building, before we even got there. He even got two cops who spoke Greek, to replace the guys watching Katarina. Of course, they knew that my young friends were on our side, so as to avoid any problems. There was a fourth guy, who took off, before everything got crazy. I don't know who he was. Sorry, I got off track. So basically it all came down to the calls. I dialed the chief and put on a show. I didn't think she was going to crack, but we got her to rat out Arthur as the killer. Once she fingered him, they gave the signal and Arthur and Hans put their double cross into play. I wish I could have seen their face when they snuck into the building to find themselves surround by New York's finest."

"How do you know that Arthur really did it? She could have been lying."

"I have to give credit to Mickey. In his notes he mentioned that Arthur smoked a rare brand of Turkish cigarette. He was smoking them while we were waiting for the Greek men to arrive, so we could drive them to the hiding place. They were the same cigarettes which had piled up at the scene. I had him, but I needed to hear it from Katarina."

Henry took a long drink of his beer. He didn't say if he needed it to make a stronger case for the DA, or just for his own piece of mind. Luna didn't ask. There were other strings which hadn't been tied up, like who killed the two guys who brought it over, or who shot Randy, but Henry didn't care. He had found the truth.

Henry and Luna sat and held hands. Nothing else needed to be said.

About the Author

The author can be found at his blog, http://ExtremelyAverage.com or on Twitter @ExtremelyAvg. His bio on Twitter sums him up well: "I have delusions of novelist, am obsessed with my blog, college football, and occasionally random acts of napping. I also Mock! Will follow cats & guinea pigs."

Reach the Author at:

Blog: http://ExtremelyAverage.com

Twitter: http://twitter.com/#!/ExtremelyAvg

Email: brian@extremelyaverage.com

G+: http://gplus.to/extremelyaverage

Facebook: https://www.facebook.com/Brian.D.Meeks

Made in the USA
Lexington, KY
13 May 2017